I0739297

The Age of Heroes

The Last Great Hero
Book 1

Scott J. Robinson

All characters and events portrayed
in this book are fictional,
and any resemblance to real people
or incidents is coincidental.

Copyright © 2014
Scott Robinson

2nd Edition

ISBN-13: 978-0-9943355-0-0

For more information visit
www.tengama.com
or email
scott@tengama.com

Cover art by
Jason Nguyen
www.jasonnart.com

Please help support
independent writers and publishers.
Your money is wonderful.
So are your reviews,
comments, mentions, tweets,
emails, blogs, likes
and deliveries of chocolate.

The Age of Heroes

Thersday

RAWK, THE LAST OF THE GREAT HEROES, wondered how long he should wait. It was a question that had been plaguing him for years, one way or the other.

"There he is..."

"He always looks smaller close up..."

"He's carrying Dabaneera...*"*

If he entered the common room too soon, not everyone would notice. If he left it too long, he would just end up looking silly. So he hesitated in the doorway, hand on the hilt of his sword, then stepped into the room. It smelled of ale and greasy meat, which was better than a lot of other taverns. Sometimes they just smelled of ale.

The owner of the *Mason's Hammer* paid Rawk a few ithel to eat in the common room every Thersday. The crowds grew as word spread and everyone was happy. Except Rawk was just about ready to move on. There was a tavern further west that did some type of foreign food that looked interesting. They might be willing to pay for his services. He held back a sigh as he moved through the crowd. Once, kings and queens had paid him to eat at their table. They'd paid him to clear exotic creatures from hunting grounds and from dungeons. Now...

He shook hands with a couple of men, returned random greetings, smiled and waved.

Normally, the table in the back corner was vacant but Weaver was sitting there this afternoon. The prince obviously thought he was being inconspicuous. It wasn't working. He was wearing a bad wig and a costume that had been rejected by second-rate street performers. Rawk completed his procession, finally letting out the sigh as he sat down. Except he *was* carrying *Dabaneera*, for some reason, and the sword was longer than his usual blade. The point jabbed the worn timber of the floor and the hilt rammed up into his kidney like a well-aimed punch. He grunted in pain, hoping nobody noticed above the general din, then stood back up and did some rearranging. The blade was stuck between two floorboards and took some freeing. Not quite the smooth, classy operation he'd been hoping for.

"Nice entry, Rawk."

"Shut up..." Rawk bit back laughter as he rubbed his side and tried to remember this weeks' name. Weaver's terrible fake accent didn't help, with either the laughter or the name. Neither did the outlandish clothes. Possibly both came from Cabalar but it was hard to tell. His red wig, clashing with his beard, sat crookedly under his floppy hat. "Nice to see you too, Gaspar." He winced at the look on Weaver's face, even as he remembered that the Prince had been 'Gaspar' last week. Oh well, too late now.

"I've already ordered, seeing you were so late."

Of course he had. Two minutes late was late enough for Weaver to take control. If there was one thing Weaver liked, it was taking control.

"That's fine." Rawk knew what the prince had ordered anyway.

Before he'd even finished the thought, a maid bought two steaming bowls of potato stew and two big chunks of bread. The woman also handed Rawk a pristine white cloth before bustling away.

"Thanks, Nibbi," Rawk called after her as he took his steel, ivory–handled spoon from one of the pouches on his belt.

Weaver grunted. "Are you *really* still afraid of being poisoned?"

Rawk had never been afraid of being poisoned. Why would anyone poison him? And if they did, why wouldn't they just put it in the food? The truth was, he just didn't like the feel of timber in his mouth. But people didn't need to know a thing like that; he had a reputation to keep. And the forks and knives found at taverns generally weren't sharp enough to stab mashed potato so he had some of them as well. A matching set that had been with him for more than ten years. "Of course I'm not *afraid*. But you can never be too careful."

Weaver leaned across the table to whisper. "That's why I only go out in disguise. The locals wouldn't harm me, but you never know who might be about." He smiled and dug into his stew with his timber spoon. Gravy dripped down his brocaded shirt.

"You do know that everyone in the city knows who you are, right? You do know that they know the two of us meet a couple of times a week?" Rawk sighed and concentrated on his food. It was a wonderful meaty stew with thick gravy and just the right amount of potato and spice.

The prince adjusted his wig, looking around to see who was watching. "Nobody knows, Rawk." He stared suspiciously at a woman eating at the next table. "They may suspect, but they don't *know*. If they knew, they would be coming to talk to me all the time." The woman passed his inspection. "The people love me too much to sit by and say nothing."

Rawk was going to argue the point, but he didn't. The people of Katamood *did* love Weaver and all that he had done for them and the city, which was why they let him have his little victories.

"I can remember when the two of us could walk through a crowd unnoticed. Except by the women, of course."

Rawk nodded, though it had never been like that. When they had started out, the women hadn't noticed them either, two skinny teenagers with rusty swords and threadbare clothes. The women only started noticing after they became famous which took a couple of years. After that...

It didn't take long for a good Hero, a skilled Hero, to become public property. And that had been almost thirty-five years ago. That was a long time. He ate some more stew. "Do you ever wish we could go back?"

Weaver sat forward in his seat and started to say something. He fiddled with his bowl, spinning it in place.

"I have actually been thinking about that recently." He sat back again and looked intently at Rawk. "I mean, what happened to us? I sit around in the palace all day balancing books and..." He waved his hand. "And princing. And you catch rats and help old ladies across the street."

Rawk didn't say anything. He'd never helped an old lady cross the street, but it was bound to happen sooner or later.

"Maybe not all the way back," Weaver continued. "I don't want to sleep under trees. Or raid chicken coops for eggs."

"Or wash dishes to pay for a room at night," Rawk added.

Weaver laughed. "Exactly. Just back to when things started to come together for us."

"Back to the glory days." *Back before my knees ached and my elbow clicked. Back to when I had hair.*

"Maybe after Falangoon? Or those mountain galangs?"

"Maybe. But it doesn't matter, really."

They both turned to concentrate on their stew.

"We could go find a dragon to kill," Weaver said eventually. He wiped gravy from his face with his sleeve. There were drops glistening on the table like still–warm blood. "There must be some somewhere."

"Nowhere near here. And we know who to blame for that, don't we?" They'd had the same conversation, in one form or another, a thousand times before. Weaver had outlawed magic, which meant there were no sorcerers who were willing to draw attention to themselves by opening ohoga portals. And if there were no portals then the supply of exots was always going to dry up. It hadn't been too bad until other rulers in the area started following suit. Now, there wasn't a land for more than five hundred miles where sorcery wasn't banned.

Weaver held up a hand and a half dozen gaudy rings flashed in the sunlight. "I know. I know. I stand by my actions, but it's still nice to dream, isn't it?" He sighed and sat back, a strange look in his eyes. "The two of us on the road like old times. Free to do what we liked when we liked. Sex whenever we wanted, with whoever we wanted. I would love to go back."

"So would I. What old man wouldn't?" He rubbed at his chin beard. He still had *some* hair.

"We aren't old, Rawk."

"This year is thirty years since you proclaimed yourself prince. Thirty years, Weaver." He shook his head as he sat back.

"Well, if I hear any rumors about dragons or any other exots, you'll be the first to know, old man."

"That would be great. Thanks."

When the flow of conversation in the room changed, Rawk looked up and saw a man from the City GFuard hurrying towards their table.

"Good afternoon, Waydin," Rawk said.

The other man tugged at his ear, as if he couldn't decide if he should acknowledge Weaver's presence or not. "Ahhh, can you come outside with me for a moment, Rawk?"

"What for? Am I under arrest?"

The crowd laughed.

"We need to talk."

By the time Rawk came with up a witty reply, Waydin had grown tired of waiting. He gave an exasperated sigh. "Something has turned up."

Rawk gave that some thought and went through several possibilities, each as unlikely as the one before. "What turned up?"

"A wolden wolf."

"Oh."

Waydin nodded. "A group of men saw it from Sparrow Tower about half an hour ago."

"Are they sure?"

"Captain Lakin was there."

Nobody was going to question Lakin's reliability as a witness. Not to his face, anyway.

"Rawk," Weaver said.

"Yes."

"I've heard a rumor about an exot."

Rawk raised his eyebrows and looked at the Prince. "Really?"

"Yes. A wolden wolf. Or so I hear."

"You don't say."

Weaver smiled. "That happened quicker than I was expecting."

Rawk turned back to Waydin. "And... You want me to go and have a look at this wolden wolf?"

The soldier's eyes narrowed as if he didn't quite understand the question. "Of course."

Rawk felt like saying, *It's only a wolden wolf,* but the crowd was watching. If this one was *only a wolden wolf* then what about all the others he'd killed? They weren't scary either? Besides, he hadn't done anything even remotely Heroic for more than a month so a nice little outing with a relatively harmless exot might be good.

"Should I go see to this beast?" he asked the audience.

They let out a cheer and most of them surged upright. Some did nothing more, but a few headed for the door, keen to find the best vantage points before they were taken.

"Right, then." Rawk managed to avoid sighing, but only by an act of will he didn't know he was capable of at that time of the day. As if he'd expected everyone to suggest he stayed right where he was and have a second course of stew. He turned back to Waydin. "Just let me..." But he already had *Dabaneera,* which had a nice long reach to get to the wolf before it closed too much. And there was nothing else he really needed. A loincloth might have been handy—people seemed to like that kind of thing—but he wasn't going to walk back up the hill just for that.

"Are you coming?" Rawk asked Weaver.

"I don't think so. I have things to do. Honey to sell. Things like that."

Halben. From Rinton. Of course. "Well, good luck with that. I'm sure I'll see you around."

Rawk wiped his spoon with the pristine white cloth and placed it back in the pouch with his fork and knife. He stood up, checked he hadn't forgotten anything, and followed Waydin out of the common room. The crowd came as well.

The procession was stymied almost before it started. Outside, a dozen dwarves were working on a deep, sheer-sided ditch that was creeping down the street. There were a few more working a handle that lifted full buckets from below ground up to the back of a waiting wagon. And there were at least a handful standing around leaning on shovels and picks. To a man, they were dirty and stank like a week old breakfast.

"Clear the way," Rawk told them, though there wasn't a lot they could do. The ditch was there now and would be until they put in the supports then laid the huge pavers over the top, then a layer of dirt, then more pavers. He could have followed the porch to the stairs at the end, but others were already heading in that direction and he didn't want to follow. He wanted to lead.

But the Gang Boss nodded and took off his wide brimmed hat to swat at some of his workers. "Won't be long here, sir. You'll be right as rain for breakfast tomorrow." They managed to clear a foot of extra space.

Rawk grunted. It would be a couple of hours at most. There was another crew just ten yards behind, lining the walls of the trench with grey slop. And ten yards behind them another work gang was closing everything back up. "You should be doing this at night when you won't be disturbing people."

"Gangs are working around the clock, sir."

Rawk knew that. He could hear them singing their strange songs at all hours. "Well, just get on with it then."

"We've been getting on with these sewers for nearly two years."

"Well…" Rawk decided to just leave before the frustration and the stench overwhelmed him. He stomped down the stairs, sidled through the gap and out into the sparse traffic.

The crowd behind him weren't as polite. They swore at the workers as the passed. One man, perhaps emboldened by the people around him, shoved a dwarf out of the way. Nobody liked dwarves, but Rawk decided everyone would complain louder if they had to do all the extra work themselves.

Despite the name, Runner Road wasn't much more than an alley that twisted and wound its way along the lower skirts of Two Watch Hill. Most of Westside was similar—quiet, narrow streets with buildings looming close on either side. The residents probably didn't appreciate the dwarves coming in with their wagons and their singing and they wouldn't appreciate a Hero and a bunch of rowdy spectators either. The *Mason's Hammer* and the surrounding buildings were three stories high with businesses at ground level and residences above. The plaster infill between the exposed frames of the half–timber walls was plain but clean and bright. The street was neat and tidy, though the dwarves were probably cleaning up any rubbish as they went.

Rawk tried to get his bearings as he made his way westward. He and Waydin eventually turned right and followed Argent Road. The crowd seemed to pulse as new people joined to find out what was going on and others grew restless with the slow pace and raced ahead to find the best spots to watch the upcoming.

A mile further on, Rawk turned away from the road, cutting down a narrow alley barely wide enough to fit his shoulders. He was on his own, now. Even Waydin had had excused himself a while earlier so he could search for the best view.

The alley ended at a small courtyard at the base of the City Wall. Except the wall didn't really protect the city. Katamood was on the outside. The wall protected the forest on the other side.

Here, the wall was nothing more than a pile of cracked brown blocks that had long ago given over to grass and weeds. Sparrow Tower stood forty yards to the north; a squat round affair that, on the other hand, looked like it was never going to fall down.

Most of the wall was like that—long lines of ruins punctuated by the occasional upright stretch—but it was part of the city's charm and allure. Katamood, the thriving city that had grown right beside the bones of some long forgotten civilization. The greatest city of the world living in the shadow of a very big, very real reminder of what could happen, what *would* happen, to everyone in the end. Or something like that, anyway. Rawk like to spin tales and wax lyrical as much as the next man but in reality he thought the ruins were just a city that was attacked and sacked and eventually died out. Nothing romantic about that. No lessons. Just life.

−O−

A rough trail lead up to a small, twisted apple tree at the top. A crow watched from the branches, talking in a harsh guttural language, complaining about something. Rawk went down the other side and a clatter of rocks followed. He didn't look back until he'd gone another thirty yards, out into a sea of thigh−high grass. Further north, the forest lapped at the wall but here it hung back from the solid grey mass of Sparrow Tower as if it was up to no good and didn't want to be caught out. There had once been dozens of towers along the five mile length of wall but now only four remained.

Up on the top of the tower, Lakin pointed more to the north. Rawk couldn't see anything interesting in that direction but that didn't mean it wasn't there.

He looked at his shirt. "Damn. I like this shirt." But there was nothing he could do about it. With a sigh, he tore open the front of the shirt, baring his chest. The crowd cheered. There must have been a thousand of them clustered around the tower and at several other spots. They seemed to make more noise than they should. Maybe he imagined it. He ripped the shirt the rest of the way off and threw it to the ground as he gave voice to a wordless battle cry. The cheering grew louder. Applause washed over him. He drew *Dabaneera* and held it aloft, saluting those who watched. And the sound of the cheering pushed him onwards as he adjusted his course and headed for the trees.

Five yards from the forest, Rawk stopped and glanced back at Sparrow Tower. Lakin gave him the thumbs up, then shrugged, as if to say 'You're in the right spot, but I can't see anything now'.

"Great." Rawk took a step towards the trees. The crowd wouldn't be able to see anything if he continued. On the other hand, they'd think him a coward if he stayed where he was. Besides which, he could be waiting for the rest of the week.

He was about to salute the crowd again, just to buy some more time, when a sound emerged from the trees. It wasn't much. A rustle of the undergrowth. A whisper from the creatures up in the branches.

Rawk took a step forward.

Then a creature emerged from the trees.

Rawk took a step back. He swallowed. "That's not a wolden wolf."

It was a wolf of some kind. Lakin had *that* right. He may just have forgotten to mention that the thing was the size of a horse. A horse with very big teeth. Rawk took another step back. He shifted his grip on *Dabaneera*. *Extra reach?* He needed a barge pole. He needed a shield. He needed some armor. He needed to be somewhere else. It was fifteen years since he fought anything like this. At least. And he was pretty sure it had hurt.

The noise of the crowd hit him again. *Are they blind?*

The wolf lowered its head and stared. It took a step towards him. It was a magnificent looking creature. All muscle and sinew. Strength and grace. Stillness and precision.

Rawk doubted running would do him any good even if the crowd left him with that option. He tried to think of what he might have done in the same situation twenty years ago. Well, firstly, he wouldn't have let himself get into the situation in the first place. The crowd at the *Mason's Hammer* had goaded him into immediate action instead of taking the time to do things properly. They hadn't actually said anything, of course, but that didn't change the facts.

Options? Every second he waited was an advantage for the wolf. The element of surprise was his best course of action. The creature knew he was there, so he couldn't surprise it *that* much, but it probably wasn't used to things that just *attacked* it. So, now or never.

Rawk flexed his hands on *Dabaneera*, took a deep breath, and rushed forward. He leapt into the air before he was within range. His sore knee almost collapsed under him. His battle cry turned into a cry of pain that he could hardly hear over the noise of the crowd. He blinked back tears.

The wolf followed his movement, looking up, eyes narrowing, teeth bared. And Rawk ducked into a roll in mid air. He hit the ground hard. More pain. His shoulder jarred and he barely managed to keep his grip on *Dabaneera*. But he held on and, rolling in close, slashed across the wolf's exposed throat.

As easy as that. Rawk congratulated himself as he rolled to his feet. He staggered as his knee took his weight. His shoulder yelled abuse.

For a moment, the wolf fought death. And in that splatter of blood–drenched time dagger–long, dagger–sharp claws raked across Rawk's arm.

A cry of pain. Again. Rawk didn't know if it was his or the wolf's. All the same in the end.

He passed out when the wolf landed on top of him, but it must have been for only a moment. The crowd still cheered. The blood still pumped out onto the ground. The pain still screamed up and down his arm. And his knee was worse. *He* was still screaming. Or he had started again.

Rawk clamped down on his fear and pain, managing to get control of his voice before anyone heard. He thought of staying put, waiting for help to arrive, but that wasn't very dignified or Heroic and the noise of the crowd started to change as they wondered if he still lived. So he put his hand on the wolf's neck, fingers sinking deep into the soft grey fur, and pushed with all his strength. He grunted with the effort, biting back more unHeroic sounds, before gravity took over and the wolf's head thumped down onto the ground.

He climbed to his feet, wavering, favoring his left knee, then had to stoop back down to collect his sword. It wasn't easy. Upright once more, he held *Dabaneera* up to the crowd and they cheered. The adulation gave him strength for a moment. But only for a moment. He crouched down then—it was either that or fall down—and looked at his arm. There was blood, and a gash, but he couldn't see a lot. He'd seen worse, he supposed. And at least it wasn't his sword arm.

He turned his attention to the exot. It definitely wasn't a wolden wolf, but he didn't know what it was. He'd never seen anything like it and hoped to never again. Soldiers were slowly making their way across from the tower. While they came, Rawk pushed his fingers into the fur again, searching. He found the buckle, cold and hard, and undid it with shaking fingers. The collar was a long strip of red leather, studded with steel. Before the soldiers came close enough to see, Rawk threw it under a bush at the edge of the forest. If they didn't see it they couldn't do anything about it. If he couldn't see it, maybe he would forget about it.

–O–

"That isn't a wolden wolf," Waydin said.

"Really?" Rawk gave his knee a surreptitious rub. It normally wasn't too bad, if he didn't do anything crazy, and he'd almost forgotten about the old injury in the last couple of months. Now that he'd injured it, it would probably hurt for the next week. He would try to avoid doing *that* again. He carefully stood up, avoiding putting too much weight on his knee, and snatched his useless shirt off the soldier. He pulled it on, torn though it was, in an attempt to hide his injured arm though nobody would see his blood through the wolf's. Even that hurt, but he tried not to show it. And getting it off would hurt even more. "I'm going to have a word with Lakin."

"It wasn't his fault."

"Really? Would you mistake a lion for a house cat?" Rawk managed to avoid looking towards where he'd thrown the collar.

Waydin ignored the question. "Where do you think it's from?"

There were a group of soldiers gathered around the wolf. None of them seemed keen to get close, though it was well and truly dead. Rawk shuddered and turned his attention to the forest. "Not from in there," he said. *Then where?*

Rawk had done a lot of travelling in the last forty years. Habon in the south to Quera in the north. Tharpin in the east to Kenkona in the west. Across two continents and more than twenty–five nations. And in all those years he'd neither seen anything like the wolf nor heard reports from a reliable person who had.

"Do you want the skin?"

Rawk shook his head. "Give it to Weaver. He likes that kind of thing."

"Did he come with you?"

"Of course not. Gaspar, or whoever he is this week, might have been in the crowd though."

Rawk didn't wait to see if the conversation had finished. He put some more weight on his sore leg and found it wasn't too bad at all, considering. So, with the crowd still watching, he sheathed his sword and walked back towards the city. He tried not to limp too much. People were starting to edge out past the wall. They cheered as he approached but parted to let him through. A Hero was all very well, but they could see him any time. A giant wolf was something else entirely. As long as the Hero had already dispatched it, of course. People patted him on the back. Others wanted to shake his hand. He gritted his teeth, smiled and pushed on.

He clambered back over the tumbled down wall, thankful for the excuse to use his hands to stay upright. Give it a few minutes and he might be doing the same thing on a perfectly good street. The crow was still in the tree on the top. It cocked its head to one side but remained silent. Perhaps *I told you so* needed no words.

At the mouth of the alley, Rawk paused to have another look at his arm but couldn't get a moment to himself. Every stranger that spotted him wanted to talk, to shake his hand, to make him a part of their day. He had three conversations about the 'wolden wolf', one about the weather and one about a giant snake he'd killed five years earlier. Before the next person could step in to take more of his time, Rawk moved away from his shady corner. He followed the road back towards the *Mason's Hammer* before turning aside and making his slow way up towards the crown of the city.

As he climbed the hill, the buildings became larger. The street was wider too, and filled with the scent of the flowers that filled small yards in front of the houses. Roses and violets. Pennylace and gerbera.

A pair of dwarves stood in the street, looking up at a window. For a moment, Rawk wondered if they were going to rob the place, then he saw that the shutters were crooked. They were probably going to repair them. That was what dwarves did.

Someone had once told Rawk that scents had different weights. So the scent of horse dung might weigh more than the scent of a rose and would therefore hang closer to the ground. So he wondered what the dwarves could smell, if not the flowers.

Rawk's mind wandered. He looked ahead and concentrated on the stone mermaid that sat atop the fountain in the Placton Square park. It rode a wave of trees. A couple of minutes later, he could see beneath the trees all the way to the coral shard on which the mermaid sat and the clam shaped cistern at the base. There were people all around it though they didn't use if for cleaning clothes or filling pots as they once had.

The park took up most of the square with just a wide road around the outside. Weaver's Palace was on the left, and opposite, on the other side of Placton Square was the *Hero's Rest*. The palace sat on the very top of the hill, but the *Rest* had the prime position. It perched atop a finger of stone that pointed southwest with views of the bay and the forest and the river that tied Katamood together. And to the west, a glimpse of the Yanandar Sea. The *Rest* was the largest inn in the city, three stories high with stables and a beer garden. It had burned down twenty years ago but been rebuilt and improved since. It was one of the few stone buildings in the city but just recently the dwarves had added new foundations and internal columns so they could build a huge water tank on the roof. Minstrels wouldn't have sung of the building's beauty before but with the tank on top it now resembled a hunchback looking for somewhere to sit. Rawk limped up onto the timber boards of the front deck.

In the taproom, a dozen human men sat at tables and at the long bar. They nursed their ales and talked quietly. Merchants, lords, soldiers. All of them knew better than to make a commotion. The last person to do so had been thrown out on his ear, with a broken arm as an added bonus, and warned to never come back. Travis, who'd done the throwing and the breaking, stood behind the bar smiling and polishing tankards. He was a big man with a face and body more suited to back alleys and barracks. Today, Mykle was with him. He was younger and bigger though as yet unproven in the area of throwing. From all the evidence, he didn't smile much at all.

Rawk nodded to the two men but didn't slow. He thought if he slowed he might topple over and never get back up.

"Can we have a word, Rawk?" Travis said.

He gritted his teeth. "What's it about?"

"Money, of course." He scratched at the scar on his neck, as he always did when he talked about money.

"Not now, then. I've got to go see somebody this afternoon"

"Later?"

"As ever." Rawk staggered and had to lean against the doorframe for a moment. He tried to rub his knee but that just hurt his arm. "I may need a hand with a couple of things upstairs in a minute, Travis, if that's all right."

Travis paused in his polishing. "Of course."

"Are you all right?" Mykle asked.

Rawk looked pointedly around the room. "I'm fine. I've just got to..." He waved his hand as he tried to think. Neither thing was easy to accomplish on its own, let alone together. "I just need some help moving some furniture."

He took a deep breath and managed to get mobile again. In the hall, he kicked the stopper away so the door swung shut behind him and nobody could see. He clutched at the wall like a drowning man clinging to the last, tiny piece of spar. He might have stayed there all day, or at least until Travis came looking for him, but noises on the stairs above forced him into action again. One of the other permanent residents made his way down the stairs.

"Good afternoon, Rawk," Natan said with a smile that filled his round, red face. "I hear you have been busy."

"Never a dull moment around here, Natan." The other man's ample girth gave Rawk an excuse to lean against the wall again as they passed. Natan once said he always wore black because it was slimming but Rawk found that hard to believe.

"I just wish you would complete your heroics closer to home. It has been many years since I saw anything exciting."

"You probably could have seen from the porch."

Natan nodded. "Oh, I could. But it was all very small and—" he waggled his fingers—"Vague."

"Well, it wasn't from close up."

Natan nodded. "I'm sure it wasn't."

"Well, I've got to get ready for an appointment."

"Of course."

Natan continued on his way. He probably wouldn't get much further than the taproom or the beer garden. That was the normal extent of his travels.

When he had gone, Rawk grunted and pushed himself into motion. He didn't bother pretending now; he leaned against the wall as he fought his way up the steps. Each was a battle worthy of any he had fought in the past. The Lion of Gaganar. Herpatos. The five Witch Sisters. The Battle of Vilanor, though that had been a dozen battles all in one. That silly snake the citizen had mentioned earlier.

Rawk lived on the top floor. It seemed he had relived half his life by the time he staggered up the last of the stairs and he wondered if a nice ground floor room might be the way to go in the future. He stopped to rest then completed the short journey to his door.

The first room wasn't much. A big bed, the blankets and sheets a continent of mountain ranges. A sword standing in the corner. A chest at the foot of the bed with a few odds and ends. Another long, flat chest under the bed with some weapons. A chest of drawers with some clothes. The only decoration was a moulting tapestry showing a trio of naked water nymphs and a very excited warrior.

Rawk managed to unbuckle his sword belt and let the weapon fall to the floor. He leaned against the tapestry for a while. It was priceless. Seven hundred years old. The last piece ever created by Lacalar. He hadn't known that when he got it. He hadn't known when he hung it on the wall. He'd taken it as loot from... well, he didn't remember... and years later a woman told him what he had. Priceless. Very soft. He wondered for a moment if he'd ever get the blood out. Rawk got himself upright with a hand on a nymph's breast and fought to push the tapestry aside. Priceless and soft and *heavy*. Eventually, he didn't so much move the tapestry aside as sidle in behind it so he could open the door that it hid and slip through, into the short hallway beyond.

Outside the first door, he paused. He was exhausted. His arm wasn't screaming at him any more. It was just numb. His whole body seemed to be numb. But that wasn't why he paused. Well, it wasn't the only reason. He paused because he didn't want to go through the door. It felt as if he was outside Habanar's Chamber again, about to go in and face the dragon.

"This is stupid." It was barely more than a whisper. He went through to face the dragon.

He hadn't seen the room since the dwarves had been there. It had just been a small storage room before, now the corner was tiled and adorned with a strange assembly of metal pipes. There was also a basin with more pipes and a seat with a fold down lid. Rawk didn't want to think about the seat. He didn't want to think about anything, so he leaned against the basin and tried to pull off his shirt. The material stuck, pulling away the drying blood and setting it flowing afresh. The arm screamed again. Leaving his clothes on, he staggered into the tiled corner and stood there, wavering as he looked at the pipes and the little handles. The taps. With a deep breath, he turned one The dwarves had told him what would happen, but he still gasped when the cool water sprayed down from above. He didn't have the energy or the balance to move clear so he leaned against the wall and let the water flow down over his face.

Such a simple thing. It felt wonderful, not like rain at all, though he wished he could get his clothes off. He watched the dirt and blood, the wolf's blood and his own, flow down the hole in the floor.

"Rawk? Are you in here?" The door opened and Travis stuck his head in. He looked at the blood flowing down the drain. "Path, what happened to you?"

"That wasn't a damn wolden wolf. It was huge. I'm lucky it didn't rip me in two." Rawk felt slightly better but could only wonder if it was just a trick of the cool, flowing water. He didn't dare try to stand upright. "I'm going to need some help."

"Why didn't you get help earlier?" Travis hurried over then paused to get his bearings. He removed his own shirt and breeches first, revealing more scars and a smooth, pink burn, then stepped under the water. He started carefully peeling the shirt away from Rawk's arm.

"I'm Rawk; the moment I go around asking for help it's all over, Travis."

"No, the moment you *die* it's all over."

"Same thing." Rawk winced as the last of the material came away from his arm. Blood swirled around his feet. "This is all I have."

"Bullshit, Rawk. You don't need to be a Hero any more. Retire. Rest. You are the last of the great Heroes. Nobody will forget you."

"Of course they will. Some new entertainment will come along and I'll just be some old man sitting in the corner of a taproom."

"And what's wrong with that? You're already half retired anyway."

Rawk just looked at him.

"I'm going to have to send for Janas."

"You're—"

Travis held up his hand before Rawk could say any more. "No, you need a proper healer."

"Well, Janas died."

Travis looked up from the arm. "What? When?"

"A couple of weeks ago."

"Well, she must have been ninety. We shouldn't be surprised, I suppose."

"I'm *not* surprised. I'm annoyed that I no longer have a healer I can trust."

Travis shook his head. "Yes, I'm sure her family are devastated for you."

"Look just get me some harawort to keep me going. I know someone I can see."

"I don't know..."

"Travis."

"Very well, but this healer had better not live too far away."

–O–

Rawk sat down on the bed wearing nothing but the fresh, clean bandages. "Thank you, Travis. I owe you one." The pain and the bleeding had both subsided. Perhaps it had all been shock. Perhaps he was just getting old. He winced as he flexed his knee as well.

"One?" Travis shook his head. "You know, for the last year I've been counting the times you said that? As of now, you owe me two hundred and seventy two 'ones'."

Rawk smiled. "Maybe, but this 'one' is worth considerably more than the 'one' I owe you from when you let me hide behind the bar to get away from..."

"Halip."

"Yes, that's her. She wouldn't take no for an answer."

"Not when you'd already said *yes* a couple of times the night before. You bring it on yourself, you know."

Rawk smiled some more. "Getting caught wouldn't have been the end of the world."

Travis threw a towel at him. "I should get going. I imagine the evening crowd has already started to arrive."

When he was alone, Rawk sighed and carefully rose to his feet. He looked around, but there weren't any clothes on the bed or floor; Travis had been busy, obviously. He went to the drawers for underwear, breeches and a long sleeved shirt to cover the bandages.

His belt lay near the foot of the bed. He removed *Dabaneera*. He leaned the weapon against the wall then thought better of it and pulled the weapons' chest out from under the bed. He found *Kult* on top and swapped it for the other blade. And he remembered he was going to see Silver Lark, so he rummaged some more. Below the swords and daggers and a mace—where the hell had he gotten a mace and why did he still have it?—were some amulets he hadn't even bothered pulling out for the last few years.

The first one had an eagle engraved onto the face. Rawk didn't know its purpose but he liked the picture. He tossed it back in the box and pulled out the next. A brass thing that was supposed to improve the taste of food. He'd never known if he should wear it or throw it in the pot. Either way, it would take more than magic to turn anything he cooked into something edible. That went back in the box too. The last one, tangled around the handle of a rapier that was as unlikely as the mace, was silver and gold with a star on the western side of an ivy circle. He hung the chain around his neck then made sure the amulet was facing the right direction and hidden under his shirt.

"Right." *Am I ready?* Sword, amulet, belt. He checked the pouches on his belt. They were all secure. "Right."

Back out the door again and carefully down the stairs to the taproom.

"How is it today?" Rawk asked, indicating the front door.

Mykle looked up from stacking tankards. "Not too bad."

"That's surprising."

A crowd of people blocked the street outside. They often did after Rawk did something heroic but, like Mykle said, it was relatively small. Forty or fifty people. They cheered as he stepped into view. A few years ago Weaver had been forced to send some Guards to conk heads and get things in order. Now only the die–hards continued to turn up. Maybe they were as tired as Rawk.

"Good afternoon." *It was almost evening.*

Before he could say anything else, the crowd started throwing things. Once it had been money from the men and flowers from the women. These days it was mainly ribbons tied to walnuts, which was just strange. It signified something or other, but Rawk had never been able to work it out, and nobody had bothered to tell him. He held up his hand and the nuts and the cheering started to slow.

"Thank you, everyone."

"I love you, Rawk," someone shouted.

"I love you, too." There was some polite laughter. "I appreciate your appreciation but if you keep doing this the inn keeper is going to throw me out. You make extra work for him when he has enough to do complaining about all the other work I make for him."

More laughter.

"So, I'll ask you again, instead of throwing—" He looked down and saw what appeared to be some underwear near his feet. "Instead of throwing things at me, make a donation to the Brothers of Granda. We all know they need walnuts and underwear more than I do."

But they weren't really listening.

"Were you scared, Rawk?"

"Of course he wasn't, you idiot."

"Do you think there are more of them?"

"What if there are more of them?"

Rawk wasn't given the chance to answer, even if he had wanted to. The questions kept coming and probably would for the rest of the day if he let them. "I have business to attend to," he said. "Thank you for coming to see me." He stepped off the porch and pushed his way through the crowd. Those closest to him were trying to make a path, but those behind were pushing closer and what resulted was a grunting, straining melee of people with no room for anyone. But Rawk was bigger than just about everyone else and *made* room. His arm hurt, but some other people would be hurting more. That was their problem.

When he broke into the clear, Rawk straightened his shoulders, checked he still had his belt, sword and amulet, and started down the hill. Some of the keener, and younger, members of the crowd were sure to follow but they would grow bored soon enough.

By the next corner there were only three boys left and Rawk called them over. He gave each of them an ithel. "Now on your way," he said, and they disappeared into the crowd of pedestrians. Rawk gave another brass coin to a beggar.

"Thank you, Rawk."

"Spend it well, Crath."

"Always do."

Rawk took a strip of dried meat from one of the pouches on his belt and chewed it as he moved on.

For most people, the journey to the river, down the long, narrow spine of the hill, wouldn't take very long, but at the first corner an old lady stopped Rawk to touch his arm and ask for his blessing. He wasn't a priest, and didn't really believe in The Great Path, but he knew passing on that information wouldn't do him any good. So, he touched the lady's cheek, mumbled something about dinner and continued on his way. Then there was an old man, a veteran of some war or another, who wanted to see his sword and talk about various weapons. That conversation took five minutes, and a boy stopped him for another two. Then the merchant and the baker and the two maids with baskets of vegetables in their hands. That last one took quite a while and left Rawk feeling good until a muvokit stopped him to talk about skinning wolden wolves. As if Rawk had ever skinned a wolf in his life.

Half an hour later, Rawk entered Old Square at the edge of the river and looked around. Factories had surrounded the square twenty years ago. A tannery had dominated the area, with both its size and its stench. Weaver had changed all that. Industry had been confined to the south of the river. Not only had the noises and smells of the businesses gone, but the dwarves had gone with them so it had been a good decision all round.

And what was left in the square was a thriving market place, like a flower garden of canvas roofs with strange nectar from a hundred places around the world. The scent of candied fruit and a hundred herbs followed him. Children giggled and chattered calling his name and darting away into the maze of stalls. The last rush of the day was underway with people hurrying to complete their business before the sun went down, so Rawk passed through to Dragon Bridge with just one small delay.

That was good news, but then, as he made his way into the stone dragon's maw and started the long climb towards the top of the creature's arched back, he found himself caught behind a group of fifty or so dwarves. They must have been working on the sewers. They weren't singing, which was good, but they smelled like a boatload of pigs. Rawk thought of pushing through, but there was hardly room enough for them and his arm was starting to ache again so he feared that any jostling might make him do something he would regret. He thought of going around, but the traffic on the other side was even worse with human laborers heading home from the factories and warehouses. So he bit his tongue and kept to the slow, steady pace.

Down below, the slow brown flow of water carried boats out towards the Bay of Kata. Dragon Bridge was the last that proper ships could fit beneath, and then it was a squeeze. The river wasn't deep enough for them for much further anyway. Sailors called out or sang as they worked at the sails or whatever else sailors worked at. Fishing trawlers nudged away from the wharves. A barge full of grain crawled further up river, slinking under the next bridge as it headed for the grain merchant's warehouses on the other side of the city.

For a while, Rawk felt the barge, being poled along by two dozen dwarves, was going faster than he was. Eventually, he saw his chance and darted around the outside of the crowd. He held his arm against his chest as he strode down the far side of the bridge. He passed the dragon's tail and stepped out onto the southern side of the river as if the creature had shat him out. He gave a grunt. The south was certainly where all the shit of Katamood had gathered.

It was at least five years since he'd been over the river. It was like stepping into another world. The city itself still looked the same, though the plastered walls weren't quite as white here and the exposed frames a little bit rougher, but there were more dwarves and elves and the dark skinned, native fermi than anyone else. Dwarves were everywhere. He didn't remember there being that many of them. They walked about as if they owned the place, loud and confident, showing none of the deference they showed on the other side of the river. Those who noticed Rawk grew quiet, but he now knew it to be a lie and it grated on his nerves. He felt like shouting at them, telling them to show the proper respect, but his arm throbbed and he wanted to get out of there as quickly as he could. So he tried to ignore everyone and get his bearings.

The industrial area was concentrated along the shoreline and swung around to the east of Mount Grace, clinging close to the water of the Bay. Mostly half–timber walls, but a few stone as well. One stone wall, large blocks fitted with barely a crack between, had graffiti painted on the side in sweeping, red letters. *Any man can think like his friends. It takes a great man to think like those he doesn't like.* And down the bottom, *Words of Wisdom.* There was a scaffold by another building with a dozen dwarves working to repair a roof.

Further away, the skirts of the mountain were taken up with homes, though he could see none of them from his position, with the last off the day's light disappearing by the moment. But which way to the home he wanted? It had been a long time since he'd been there...

"'Scuse me, Mr Rawk, sir."

Rawk turned and discovered a dwarf by his side. Rawk didn't know how to judge the age of dwarves but this one was even shorter than usual and didn't have a beard, so it was probably a young child.

"I'm not giving you any money," Rawk said. He almost pushed the boy away but thought better of it. Others were watching and stories travelled through Katamood faster than diseases. There were even a few humans still about.

"I don't want any money, Mr Rawk."

Rawk found that hard to believe. The boy wore not much more than rags and smelt like he'd slept in a garbage bin. His red hair stuck up all over the place.

"I thought you looked lost, Mr Rawk. I know all the places around here."

Rawk looked around. "I'm sure you do."

"Do you need some help?"

Rawk sighed. "I'm looking for..." But he didn't even know what name she was using. Surely not her own. "I'm looking for a healer..." But the very reason he sought her was because he didn't want anyone to know he needed a healer.

The boy's eyes narrowed. "There are healers over the other side of the river."

"I know. I'm getting some advice for... a friend. He doesn't like crowds but is willing to pay for the best. He gave me a healer's name but I can't remember it." Any half intelligent person would jump to the conclusion that the 'friend' was Weaver. But he *was* talking to a dwarf child, so who could tell?

The boy smiled and nodded, as if that cleared everything up. "Sylvia's the best healer in Katamood," he said. "Maybe in the whole world."

"Sylvia?"

"Just a guess."

It sounded about right. And she probably would go around telling everyone she was the best healer in the world. Rawk waved his hand into the growing darkness of the city. "Well, if you can tell me the way..." He started to reach for some money.

"I can *show* you the way. I'm Clinker." The boy bent down and collected a tattered leather satchel from near his feet. It rattled and clanked as he slung it over his shoulder. "Come on."

"Well, thank you, but..." He didn't want to be seen spending more time with a dwarf than was necessary but Clinker had already strode away through the crowd, if dwarf children could stride. Rawk hurried to catch up.

"You don't visit us much," Clinker said when Rawk fell in to step beside him.

"Not a lot of reason to—"

"Kikum said you were going to come and get rid of our grespan rats. They were about twice as big as the ones on the other side of the river, I think." He held his hands out like a fisherman describing his catch. He could barely hold them far enough apart.

Rawk grunted. "I can't do everything."

"That's what *I* said." Clinker turned down a side street. Not much more than an alley with buildings crowding close. "Anyway, Thacker organized someone to sort it out."

"Thacker?"

"Yeah, he got some workers from the wharves to go have a look, I think. Took 'em a couple of days but they got it done. They reckon they found a whole big nest of them."

"Well..." Rawk hadn't found much at all on the other side of the river. He'd traipsed around in alleys and slums for about a week killing the vile creatures and then they'd stopped coming. He hadn't argued.

"I... I was led to believe the healer lived on Mount Grace."

"She does."

"Then why are we going this way?"

Clinker laughed. "Can't go in no straight line these days, you see. It's the canal."

"Oh, right."

"They're building bridges quick smart, but they can't build them where they're still working on the canal. There's only sixty yards to go now, you know. I paced it out the other day. Me and Kikum. He says it's fifty yards, but I know it's sixty."

"Right."

A few blocks further on, Rawk stopped outside the biggest construction site he'd ever seen. He'd been watching from the *Hero's Rest* as the canal crept through the city, the leading end moving ever closer to a little stub of canal that projected out from the Bay of Kata, but to see it close up was quite another thing.

"Ain't it something?"

Ugly and noisy and dusty was what it was.

"Thacker thinks it might be the biggest engineering job ever."

Rawk grunted. "You could have gone around the other side of the mountain instead of ruining the city." Though, admittedly, cleaning up south of the river might have been a good idea.

"They was going to, but the ground was too hard. All rocks over that way. Thacker could've worked it out, but Prince Weaver didn't want to wait."

Rawk grunted again. Weaver couldn't wait for an egg to boil.

"That's what Larsi says, anyway. Not sure if I believe her though. She's just a girl."

"Can't trust them girls."

"Right." Clinker nodded and smiled.

Rawk looked at the canal as he started to walk again. From the Yanandar Sea to the Bay of Kata. Twenty miles long? It was fifty yards wide, more than enough for two ships to pass. That was a lot of dirt and rock and digging. And as far as Rawk was concerned, it wasn't going to be worth it. That was if it even worked. Weaver said he had it all worked out, but what did he know about engineering? There were hills in the way. And he knew for a fact that the tide levels in the Yanandar Sea and the Bay of Kata were different. In the end, it would just be another sewerage drain dividing the city. One that would never have stones laid back over the top. And in the meantime, there were dwarves everywhere.

A few minutes later and they came to a new bridge. There were towers on either side of the canal and a flat, broad bridge between.

"This is just stupid. You'd be lucky to get an empty barge under this thing."

"They folds up like two big draw bridges." Clinker used his arms to demonstrate again. There's going to be other bridges too. Different types. And maybe some tunnels."

Rawk shook his head in disbelief. Tunnels under the canal? Weaver always did have a problem knowing when to stop.

There was another message scrawled on the closest of the towers. *For one noble to fall, a thousand peasants must rise. Words of Wisdom.*

There were half a dozen dwarves staring up at the words. They talked for a moment, nodding and pointing, then took up buckets and scrubbing brushes and set to work.

Rawk and Clinker joined the flow of traffic and by the time they reached the tower the words were half gone. *A thousand peasants must rise.* Over the other side, they were swept back towards the mountain. Not long later they started to climb and soon the road was so steep that it became a wide, shallow flight of stairs.

"There's roads that wagons can get up," Clinker said. He seemed to have an endless amount of energy. Maybe that was the natural condition of young boys. "This way is the quickest though." The dwarf's little legs carried him along quickly but he had to jump up the stairs. His bag rattled and clanked all the way. The noise was starting to annoy Rawk as much as the back alley stench.

Rawk had trouble keeping up. His knee hurt more with every step and his arm was moving on to whatever came after a dull ache. He didn't want to know the details. "What's in the bag?"

Clinker clutched the bag tighter. "Everything."

Rawk shook his head. "Is that where you got your name? All the rattling and clinking?"

He gave it some thought. "Maybe. I don't know. I'll have to ask Kikum."

There were as many stone and brick buildings as any others now, solid, blocky things that seemed about as exciting as rain on market day. Typical dwarvish construction. No imagination. No... artistry. They probably did the job beautifully, but that was the only beautiful thing about them.

"Everyone says Sylvia's about the best healer there is," Clinker said.

"I imagine she is." Rawk continued on for a few steps after the boy stopped.

Clinker turned and gestured to a door. "She's in there. She might not be *there* though." He shrugged.

The door was unmarked. There was no sign. There was no indication that a healer worked within. "Are you sure?"

"Course I'm sure. Sylvia helped Larsi last year when she got sick. She almost died. I ran up here in the middle of the night to get her. Sylvia that is, not Larsi." He scratched at his head, messing up his hair even more.

"Right." Rawk pulled a coin from the pouch on his belt and held it out to the boy. "Don't tell anyone where you brought me, all right? My friend doesn't want anyone to know."

Clinker's eyes went wide. "Five ithel? Thank you Mr Rawk, sir. I won't tell anyone."

Rawk knew it was pointless. Dwarves couldn't be trusted at the best of times, but a boy? Clinker rattled off down the street leaving Rawk on his own.

After the dwarf had gone on his way, Rawk stared at the door. He didn't want to go in, but he needed a healer who wouldn't talk, and he didn't know of any others. He sighed and went inside. The door knocked against a bell and a familiar voice emerged from beyond a second door.

"I'll be there in a moment."

Rawk almost hurried back out the door. He didn't reply.

From the outside, there may not have been any indication of what the premises was used for, but inside there could be no doubts. He looked at one of the shelves. Corrydart. Hemlock. Bardeegood. Murtle bug shells. Across the other side, near a small counter, were jars with labels like, 'Cold', 'Headache', 'Liver Spots' and 'Lice'. Bitter and sweet, acidic and smooth, soft and sharp, a hundred different odors seemed to hang in the still air with the dust motes. Rawk sat on a stool near the counter, one hand resting on his lap, near his dagger, the other holding the amulet under his shirt. He was ready. As ready as he could be.

The voice came again. "You only just caught me." A woman came around the corner wiping her hands on a green cloth. "I was about to close up for..." She stopped in the doorway, mouth open, hands stilled, when she saw Rawk.

"Hello, Silver Lark. How are you?" He tried to sound casual, but he wasn't sure if it worked. Silver Lark had spent a lot of years trying to kill him and he didn't know if today was going to be any different.

She stood for long moments. Rawk could almost see the thoughts chasing through her head. Eventually, she cleared her throat and finished wiping her hands. She still didn't come through the door.

"It has been a long time since I heard that name, Rawk."

He licked his lips. "Should I call you Sylvia?"

"I would prefer you did. I assume Weaver does not know of my presence or he would be here himself."

"With a whole troop of Guards, I imagine."

"Of course. Though you might come on your own if the reward was high enough."

Rawk laughed though his heart pounded. "If I was after a reward, I'd have more than a dagger."

Sylvia raised an eyebrow. "A dagger and an amulet that has barely a trickle of power left. Do you think they will save you?"

Rawk shrugged and released the amulet. He watched her even closer than before but the fact that he'd made it through the initial exchanges made him think he wasn't about to die. It was hard to relax anyway. He resisted the urge to wipe sweat away from his forehead, mainly because there was none there. It just felt like there should be.

"So, to what do I owe the pleasure, after fifteen years?" She didn't look pleased. She looked wary.

"Closer to seventeen. And it shows. You're starting to look old, Sylvia." She wasn't. She looked surprisingly good. Still slim and tall, with high cheekbones and a perfect nose. It looked like she hadn't aged at all, but he wasn't about to tell her that.

"Why thank you. A gentleman as always."

Rawk couldn't remember ever having an actual conversation with her before. "No, that's a compliment. You should know that sorcerers don't get any respect until they're old and crotchety. Especially women. Who trusts a young witch to do anything right?"

"Are you calling me a witch?"

Rawk looked around the room. He didn't want to offend her, he was quite happy to still be alive, after all, but... "Potions? Really?"

"You're asking me for help and you still think you can lecture me on how far I have fallen?"

That one struck home. Rawk winced and cleared his throat. "Weaver doesn't actively look anymore."

"I know. So I'll just make my potions and keep quiet."

Rawk tensed as she came into the room and went around behind the counter.

"You're looking old too," she continued. "And, last I checked, that *isn't* a good thing for a Hero."

"Nobody cares how old merchants are, and the age of heroes doesn't matter either. As long as I can do the job."

"Can you? Most old heroes know when to retire and slip away quietly with their loot."

"Unlike me, you mean."

"Exactly. You've survived a long time so perhaps it's time to stop pressing your luck."

"Friendly advice?"

She grimaced. "Well, let's call it advice. You haven't tried to stab me yet, but let's not throw away forty years of enmity on a whim."

"At least you'll get a warning. Apparently my amulet won't help at all."

She shrugged. "You choose sorcerers as enemies and you face the consequences."

Rawk watched as she tapped her finger on the counter, as if each little movement could signal an attack. "Well, let me just make it clear—I've known you were here for about ten years and haven't once tried to kill you." Now that he thought about it, she'd known where he was as well. He relaxed. A bit.

"So why *are* you here then?"

And suddenly, Rawk was reluctant. He'd spent most of his life hating Silver Lark. And fearing her. He'd hated and feared all sorcerers, but Silver Lark in particular, and now he intended to ask her for help.

"We've known each other too long for this, Rawk. Who do you think I will tell?"

She was right. She was keeping a low profile and unlikely to draw attention to herself, which was why he'd decided to come to her in the first place. He sighed and rolled up his sleeve. The bandages were soaked in blood. There had been pain for quite some time but the tension of talking with Sylvia had kept his attention.

The sorceress raised her eyebrows. "A wolden wolf did this to you? You really *do* need to retire."

"It wasn't a wolden wolf."

She came back around the counter and started to unwrap the wound. "Really? That's what they all say."

"It was bloody huge. At least—"

"I know, Rawk." She held up a hand. "Now hold still. Thacker had some people watching. Jod was surprised *anyone* could mistake the creature for a wolden wolf."

Rawk grunted. "Exactly." He gritted his teeth against the pain as Sylvia completed revealing the wound on his arm.

"This doesn't look good. Jod said it was the size of a horse."

Rawk could only nod.

"And he says you just charged in and attacked it."

Rawk nodded again.

"Why? If you insist on continuing with this Hero business, perhaps you should at least admit your advancing years and give matters some thought from time to time."

"I did think about it. I thought about running, but that would've gotten me killed."

"You thought about running? Maybe not completely stupid after all, though I imagine the audience had as much to do with your decision to fight as did the fear of death."

Rawk hurried on. "And I thought that if the fight lasted more than a couple of seconds I'd be dead. I had to end it quickly, so I did."

"Luckily."

"Maybe."

"You really are too old, Rawk. Being a Hero is a young man's game."

"So I've been told. But I don't have anything else."

"That's what *I* thought. Now look at me." Silver Lark gestured around the room. After a moment, she laughed.

Rawk smiled. "You know, I don't think I've ever heard you laugh before."

"Apart from the maniacal kind in the midst of battle, of course."

"Of course." Rawk looked at his arm. It didn't look good. "So, what's the verdict?"

"Let me get my needle and thread. The wound itself isn't a problem—about ten stitches should fix that—but there could be infection."

When she came back, Rawk winced. "Can't you just..." He waggled his fingers.

"Magic? You can't be serious. If I was willing to give myself away, do you really think you would be the person I'd do it for? The last time we interacted, you were trying to kill me."

"Are you sure?"

"What else would you have been doing? It was at Maradon."

Rawk smiled. "That's right. The rebellion thing. King said—"

"Rebellion thing? Otherwise known as a peasant uprising. They were being taxed out of their homes in the longest drought in recorded history. They—"

"Semantics."

"Those people needed help, Rawk. *They* needed a Hero. They got me instead. King Terwin needed a conscience and he got warriors."

"I won though. The King won."

"Really? Most of the peasants that survived were forced to flee."

"No big loss."

"No big loss? Maradon's economy still hasn't recovered."

Rawk thought of pointing out that the Chancellor had embezzled away half of the country's wealth during the revolt. That was what Terwin had told him, anyway, as part of the reason he couldn't pay the agreed sum... What if the exodus of peasants had been the real problem? Rawk kept his mouth shut.

Sylvia started stitching the wound and wasn't being gentle about it. "You will *not* be getting any magic out of me." When she finished she disappeared into the back room for a moment and returned with a fresh bandage. She slapped it down into his hand.

"*I* have to do this?"

"Yes. Later." She collected two items from the shelves. "Firstly though, you soak some of this in boiling water, then drain the water off and pack the leaves onto the wound for about half an hour. Can you sit still for that long?"

"Yes. What is it?"

"It's called tea. It's from Frenable. After half an hour you throw the leaves out and you sprinkle this powder on the wound before bandaging it."

Rawk started to stand.

"What drugs did you take before?"

"Travis gave me some harawort."

"Harawort? Really? Beena taught him better than that." She shook her head and gestured to the tea again. "After you've soaked the tea, don't throw out the water. Put your head over the bowl and cover both with a towel or something so you are breathing in the steam."

"Breathing the steam?"

"That will help counteract the harawort. It will take the pain away for a while and let you get some sleep, at least."

"What about tomorrow?"

"Do it again in the morning, but I suggest you don't do anything strenuous for a week, at least."

"That won't be possible."

"Then ignore all my advice and I hope the infection kills you."

"You probably poisoned the needle anyway. This is probably the best chance you ever had."

"Seventeen years is a long time to hold a grudge, Rawk. Any animosity I felt is long gone."

"So you don't want to kill me?"

Sylvia sighed. "I never wanted to kill *anyone*. Not even you."

"Then what were we doing all those years?"

"I was trying to survive. I was trying to help people. And you were this mythical figure that came along every now and then to disrupt my plans. Like bad weather or something. For me, it was not personal. I didn't even know you."

Not personal? He'd hated her. He'd wished every sort of horrible death upon her. At the time it had felt like Silver Lark was there every time Rawk tried to do something but, when he thought about it, they had probably only battled a dozen times in all those years. And some of those confrontations hardly counted as battles at all. He didn't know what to say, so he shrugged.

Sylvia picked up the tea and the powder and held them out to him. "Take them or leave them. Either way, leave. I still have people to see tonight."

Rawk sighed and took the packages. "Thank you, Silver Lark." It felt strange to say it.

She grunted. "I suppose you'll be back next time you're injured."

Rawk didn't know if that was an invitation. "Probably."

She shooed him out the door but didn't tell him to stay away. Invitation it was.

–O–

Rawk sat up when Travis came in the door carrying a large copper bowl and a bucket of steaming water.

"So, where do you want this?" Travis said. "And why do you want it?"

Rawk looked around. There weren't a lot of options. The bowl would soon be too hot for his lap. "Just put it on the floor." He pointed vaguely and assumed Travis would work it out.

"Now what?"

"I'll do it." But Travis just stood looking at him. So he picked up the bag of tea and threw it to him. "I need some of that soaked and drained. I'm going to pack it onto the wound for a while."

Travis did as asked, working in silence.

"Do you know the healer, Sylvia? Over near Grace?"

"Of course. Everyone who has anything to do with healing does. Is that who you went to see?"

"She said you should have known better than to give me harawort."

He glanced up. "You asked for it, remember?"

"So how does she know you?"

Travis shrugged. "Maybe she keeps track of all the healers. Just so she can complain when we make mistakes." He started pressing the damp leaves into the wound. He wasn't being any more gentle than Sylvia had, so Rawk took over. "I'll throw out the water."

"Don't." Rawk told him what to do and by the time he was done with his arm the bowl was ready to go.

"And you breathe in the steam?" Travis said.

"Apparently." Rawk knelt on the floor, careful of his arm, and put his head over the bowl. Travis laid a towel over his head so it hung down to the floor with the bowl beneath.

"And that's it? What's it supposed to do?"

"Counteract the harawort, or something." He breathed in the strong, sweet smell of the tea. "Not sure I believe her though."

But even as he said it, Rawk could feel his head starting to clear. He wasn't very comfortable, kneeling on the floor, back arched, but he started to relax. His muscles seemed to loosen of their own accord. The aching of his head receded ever so slightly. The tea was helping his arm, though whether it was the poultice on it's own or the fumes as well, he couldn't tell. He waved his good arm at Travis.

"Just leave me for a while, will you. I'll be down for dinner soon."

Fifteen minutes later, Rawk sprinkled the powder on his arm then strapped it as tight as he could before making his way down the stairs. He didn't feel like he could fight of a wolden wolf, not even a real one, but he felt like he could eat one. He sat in his dark, quiet booth at the back of the common room and less than a minute later a plate piled high with roasted pork and vegetables was set down in front of him. Tasi didn't even slow. Her arms were piled high with bowls and plates.

Rawk ate as if he'd missed lunch and was glad when some bread and jam materialized as if by magic. It came with a tall silver tankard. He had time to shout, "Thanks," this time before Tasi was gone again.

He savored every bite of the bread then picked up the tankard and sat back to relax and survey the room. Someone near the door was watching him. People watched him wherever he went, it came with being a Hero, but sometimes it was different. He smiled, raised his tankard and took a sip as the girl confidently made her way across the room.

"Hello," she said, leaning against his table. "I'm Adalee."

"Hello, Adalee. I'm Rawk."

"I know who you are."

Rawk sighed. "I know you know who I am, but it feels rude to not introduce myself."

"Oh. Sorry."

"That's all right. What can I do for you tonight?"

She raised a plucked eyebrow and looked him up and down. "I don't know. But I'm sure you can think of something."

43

Faraday

RAWK SAT ON THE EDGE of the bed and catalogued his aches and pains. Arm, knee and back. Not as bad as he would have expected.

Adalee couldn't be blamed for the knee or the arm, but the sore back was all her fault. There was movement behind him and he turned to look at the girl. She sat up, sheet clutched to her breasts, much more demure than she'd been the night before. Several times. He turned away from her and tried to soak up the last calm moment he was likely to see that day.

But she was just a girl. How old had she said? Nineteen? Twenty? Not old enough to know. He felt her arms slide around him from behind and she nibbled his ear. "Shall we dance again before breakfast, my Hero?"

Rawk sighed. "You won't be having breakfast, Adalee. At least not with me."

"What do you mean?"

"You should get your things and go."

"You... But..."

Rawk turned to look at her. "What did you think was going to happen?"

"You can't treat me like one of your tavern sluts, Rawk. I am Adalee Dan Beketh. If my parents—"

"Wait? What? Who?"

The girl looked a bit smug. "That's right. My father is Edwin Dan Beketh and if he hears—"

"You'll tell your father?"

"Well..."

But Rawk didn't care about her father. "How old did you say you were?"

The sudden change of topic confused her. "I will celebrate my twentieth name day in four weeks."

Rawk tried to think. He tried to calculate. Melia Dan Beketh? The two headed snake, what a crock that had been, or the giant bear thing? He couldn't remember; it had been so long ago. And even if he knew if it was the snake or the bear, how long ago had *they* been? Maybe

Weaver would know. He sighed again. "Go home to your mother, girl."

He turned to watch as she flounced from the bed and made her way around the room collecting her clothes. He had to admit, she was beautiful, and it had been fun. The first time had been fun. Even the second. After that it had just been hard work. When she had laced her shirt up over her breasts Rawk thought he should do something about finding his own clothes. But she paused on her way out the door.

"You'd think a man like you would have more in his life than..." She looked around and gestured at the room. "Than this."

Rawk looked as well. He shrugged. "So people keep telling me. Apparently I'm supposed to grow up."

"Maybe this frugal, monk−like existence impressed women when you were my age, but now it's just sad." Adalee huffed and slammed the door behind her.

Rawk winced. "That went well." He thought he might well have a visit from Melia in a couple of days. It was years since he'd even seen her so that would be nice.

Rawk wondered if he should do something about redressing his arm when there was a knock at the door.

"Yes?"

Travis came in with a jug of hot water and a large copper bowl. Again. "I saw Adalee leaving."

"You knew who she was?"

"Of course."

"You didn't tell me."

"I assumed you would ask her."

"Well... Was she going quietly?"

Travis laughed. "Do you want to do a fresh poultice or just, you know, breathe?"

Rawk worked the muscles in his arm. "A bit of poultice, I think. But I was going to do some more of the breathing thing too. It really cleared my head yesterday and, seeing I drank a bit too much last night, I was hoping it would work again."

While Rawk worked at the bandage, Travis set about organizing the bowl. He cleared his throat but didn't look up. "I'm not going to be working tonight," he said.

Rawk raised an eyebrow though the other man still wasn't looking. "You aren't? It's Faraday, isn't it?"

"It is."

"You always work on Faraday."

"Normally, yes." Travis started working on the poultice. "Can't trust anyone else."

"So..."

"There's a show on at the Veterans' Club. I thought I'd go to see it."

"A show? You?"

"Yeah. What of it? I can see a show if I want."

Rawk held up a hand. "Of course you can. Do whatever the hell you want."

"I was going to ask somebody..."

Rawk raise the other eyebrow. "Oh. Right."

"Only..."

"No. There's no 'only'. You're too old to be waiting. At your age if you stand still too long you fall over dead. I'm sure I heard that somewhere. Sylvia would know. You do it, Travis. That's an order. Ask whoever it is and have a great time."

"Do you think?"

"Get out of here, I've got some breathing to do."

Rawk shoved his head under the towel and listened to the other man leave. Travis was just a couple of months older than Rawk. Was he too old to be waiting? Too old to be standing still?

Do you think? Not as often as I should, apparently.

Rawk kept his head under the towel for a few minutes. It did help, but he had too much on his mind for it to calm him as it had the night before. With a sigh his sat up and looked around.

His trousers were at the end of the bed. His shirt was in the corner, but it was almost torn in half. He remembered something about that but the details were lost amidst a flurry of thighs and breasts and eager hands.

He donned some new clothes, threw a cloak over the top, collected his sword and headed down stairs.

−O−

No strenuous activity for a week? Who was she kidding?

After breakfast, Rawk wandered out to the front of the *Hero's Rest*. The Faraday Festival was in full swing in Placton Square. Hawkers were calling their wares as people wandered beneath the trees, moving from performance to performance or pausing to watch roving entertainers. There were singers and jugglers, mimes and impressionists. Bubbling laughter and noise filled the air. Cafes around the outside of the square were doing a roaring trade, serving spiced wine and sparkling ale.

Rawk rubbed his knee as he watched the people passing by, returning greetings but trying not to get involved. He sat on the step. Anyone else who did the same thing would have been chased away by whoever was serving in the common room at the time, but he was Rawk, the greatest of the great Heroes.

Greatest of the great Heroes? What did that mean? A few years ago he could have told you but now he wasn't so sure. It meant the City Guard came to him when a wolden wolf needed killing instead of just going and doing the job themselves. He knew that much. It meant people thought it was all right to ask him for money at any time of the day or night. He knew that, too. With a sigh, Rawk reached into his money pouch and held out a coin for the young, raggedly dressed boy who watched him from not far away. The boy hadn't asked for money, but smiled and darted forward. He nodded his thanks as he took the coin then disappeared down the street.

It had been worse years ago, of course. The Age of Heroes was passing, drifting away into history like the Age of Gods had before, so those last few men and women plying their trade did not garner the interest they once had.

Rawk threw his pebble at an iron ring set into the cobbles, the only evidence that the dwarves had been through the area digging their damn sewerage drains. Hundreds of dwarves doing hundreds of hours of work all over the city, and soon, that ring and others like it would be all that was left to remember what had been done. The rings and the shower upstairs. And the tap in the kitchen. And...

"Path." Rawk rose to his feet and looked around, as if a great deed might be waiting to be done right there in front of him. An old man dropped a bag of apples but before Rawk could even think to help, a girl started to gather up the fruit. Rawk swore again. "The last of the great Heroes."

He pulled some dried meat from his belt and chewed as he walked down the hill towards the river. He could see the canal construction zone beyond that. As Clinker had said, there was one small section left to dig. Fifty or sixty yards of dirt and stone, depending on who you asked, was all that stood between the Yanandar Sea and the Bay of Kata.

Lost in thought, wondering what to do with himself that didn't involve anything strenuous, Rawk turned at the next intersection. It was some time before he took notice of his location. The street was narrow and looked as if it hadn't seen the light of day in years. The buildings were three stories high with balconies reaching out overhead. Clotheslines crisscrossed what was left of the sky, full of clothes that sent a patter of rain down to the worn cobbles. Someone, somewhere, was baking bread.

He'd never been here before. Five minutes walk from home and he'd never seen this place. An old lady sat on a step peeling carrots with quick easy strokes. She smiled and nodded. "Rawk." But she didn't jump up to get a blessing or talk about wolden wolves, though it looked like she could have done with the former.

"Good morning, ma'am."

The woman laughed, though if at the idea of a good morning or at being called ma'am was impossible to tell. The sounds echoed around the narrow space. Up above, a crow landed on a clothes line, squawking and flaring its wings as its new perch swung and danced beneath it. Big drops of water came down in long, slow arcs.

Rawk grunted and kept walking.

At the next corner an even narrower street ran off at an odd angle. There was no room for balconies or clotheslines. There was just a thin line of blue above the black line of cobbles. Rawk didn't like the look of it and was about to move on when he heard a scream. And a second later, someone yelled, "Fire."

Huh! There were deeds to be done. Perhaps. He had to decide where the shout had originated. There were three possibilities and nothing to give him a hint. After an agonizing moment, Rawk thought to look up again and saw a trickle of smoke drifting overhead. He turned right and ran. A hundred yards on, after pausing at two more intersections to look some more, he came to a halt in a small square near a burning building. The exposed frame at the front was already black and smoldering and the plaster between was cracked. Flames were flickering out the second floor window. A small group of people were standing not far away, waving away smoke, chattering as they watched.

Another woman wailed, wringing her hands and looking up at the window. When she looked down, she wailed even louder and raced to Rawk. She grabbed his hand. "My mother is inside," she said. "You must help her."

Rawk looked up again. The building was well alight and it could collapse at any moment. The fire was already spreading. He didn't know that he *must* do anything. His heart raced. His palms were sweating just at the thought of doing *anything*. It felt as if the smoke was gathering on his tongue, sucking the moisture from his mouth.

"You must help her."

Rawk swore but dropped his sword belt to the ground and ran to the door. He lashed out with his boot but it had no effect. Despite the flames, the door still stood strong. So he reached out carefully and lifted the lock so he could push the door open. A shower of sparks came out the gap, quickly dwindling away to nothing. Covering his face with his arm, little good that it would do, Rawk ducked inside. The heat was terrifying. He thought he could feel his skin peeling away from his face and hands. He almost retreated, but there were people waiting outside, watching.

He looked around instead, trying to remain calm. A kitchen and sitting room down stairs with a burning table and a sturdy bench that looked like it might survive for a while yet. As Rawk had feared, there was nobody waiting to be rescued. He swore again, louder this time, seeing nobody could hear, and headed for the stairs. He stayed to the side, hoping they would hold. The first floor landing led to two doors, both closed, as the stairs continued up. Door on the left, an empty bedroom that was alive with flames but not with people. Another bedroom on the other side and an old woman lying in the middle of the floor, screaming and wailing twice as much as her daughter had been outside. Flames were climbing the walls and racing back and forth across the floor. He expected it to collapse at any moment.

Rawk didn't know how the old woman still lived but did wonder if she would appreciate being rescued, even if he could get to her. Living with burns...

But that wasn't for him to decide. Taking a deep breath that scorched his mouth, Rawk darted into the room and crouched by the woman's side. She looked up at him when he touched her arm but didn't stop screaming.

Rawk swatted flames from his breeches as he wondered if going out the window would be the better option.

He started to lift the woman, painful though it would be for everyone involved, when he saw movement from the corner of his eye. In the burning room, everything moved, but this thing seemed to move against the flow of the flames. When he spotted it again, Rawk gasped.

A creature, no more than a foot high and seemingly made from flames, danced, twirling and leaping from the bed to the floor and back again.

"What in Path's name..."

There was a jug and basin on the small table beside the bed. Rawk raced to the table. Using his sleeve to cover his hand, he took up the jug. It was empty. The basin was full though and he used his other hand to snatch it up without even thinking. The metal was cool to the touch.

Bells clanged outside while the exot danced, oblivious to everything around it. Rawk threw the water, flinging it from the bowl.

The creature looked, horrified expression on its flickering face. It coughed and spluttered. And with each paroxysm the flames in the room flickered and died, just a little. Finally, after being hit with a particularly violent cough, the exot winked from existence. The flames went with it. One moment they were there, the next they were gone. The old woman wailed and, outside, the bells rang.

Rawk wished they would all shut up.

He crouched beside the closest of the annoyances.

"Hello." He touched the old lady on the shoulder but she writhed and screamed louder. It was understandable, in a way; he was only just starting to get himself under control. He took a deep breath and the scent of a thunderstorm filled his nostrils.

A few seconds later the woman opened her eyes. Her screams died away to whines, then to nothing as she looked around the room. "Did you do that?" she asked.

Rawk looked around too. "I think I might have."

"How?"

He shrugged. "I don't think there was any fire at all." He remembered the cool metal of the water bowl. "I think it was just a sprite or demon or something making us think there was a fire."

"And you killed it?"

"I threw water on it. That's all I know."

Rawk help the woman to her feet and then preceded her down the stairs. Outside, a huge crowd had gathered. And there was a horse–drawn water tank with a dozen dwarves sitting on top and clinging to the side, getting them above the press for a better view. They all cheered when Rawk stepped out through the door. The old woman hobbled over to speak with her daughter. They both sobbed while Rawk reclaimed his belt. He checked the pouches for his cutlery, money, and all the other odds and ends he carried.

"Excuse me, Mr Rawk, sir."

Rawk looked down at the dwarf. "What?"

"It looked like there was a fire."

"Yes."

"The whole building was engulfed."

"No."

The dwarf looked confused. "But you said..."

"I agreed that it *looked like* there was a fire, I never said there *was* a fire. Who in Path's name are you?"

"I'm Fallow, Captain of Station Five"

Rawk's face must have shown his confusion.

"The fire brigade."

Rawk was still confused.

Fallow sighed. "We have a tanker full of water and if there's a fire we get there as quickly as possible and try to put it out."

Rawk looked at the wagon. "You think that little bit of water will put out fires?"

The dwarf shrugged. "Probably not. But once Thacker gets the water organized we'll be able to make a difference."

Thacker again. Rawk was going to have to find out who Thacker was and what he was up to.

Fallow scratched his head. "So, it looked like there was a fire, but there wasn't really?"

Rawk nodded.

"It looked real."

"I know. It felt real, too. But nothing else was hot, just me. There was a fire sprite or something in there. Some exot that made us all think there was a fire."

The dwarf nodded. "So, the wolden wolf, or whatever it was, and now this fire sprite thing."

"What of it? They aren't related."

Fallow shrugged. "I'm not suggesting they arrived at the station on the same train or anything. But we get no such creatures for months—"

It had been years, actually, but Rawk was still trying to work out what a *train* was.

"—and now we have two in two days? I guess I just think it's a bit of a coincidence, that's all."

"Whatever. They're both dead."

"Well, I guess we aren't needed then."

"No. So go back across the river."

"Got four hours left on my shift yet, Mr Rawk."

Rawk shook his head and walked away.

A coincidence? Maybe, maybe not, but it didn't really matter. Not when there were huge not-wolden-wolves wearing collars. He swore and flexed his sore arm. *No strenuous activity for a week?* His knee complained already.

Satyrday

RAWK BREATHED IN THE TEA while the poultice worked on his arm.

"A fire sprite?" Travis asked.

"Well, I don't know if that was its proper name," Rawk replied.

"Two in two days?"

"I know, and there's something I want to go and look at this morning."

"Well, it looks like business is picking up for you."

Rawk grunted. "I don't know how long this will last. Weaver will probably make it a law that exots aren't allowed to appear at all, even if they don't have the help of sorcerers."

"And I'm sure they'll all listen."

"Everyone else seems to. Do you really think the canal and the sewers are going to work?"

Travis shook his head. "I'd say the sewers are already working. You've got running water right next door. And if you ever work up the courage you can use the crapper instead of making me carry around your buckets of shit."

"When was the last time you carried a bucket of shit?" Rawk finally pushed away the towel and sat up.

"Do you know what we do with the buckets of shit now?"

"No. And I don't want to."

"We pour them in the sewer, Rawk."

"And what happens to it then?"

"It flows down to sea."

"I swim in that water."

"You do not. And anyway, apparently the pipes go so far out that the crap gets washed further out to sea without ever getting close to shore."

"It does? How do you know?"

"You saw them laying the pipes."

"All I saw was dwarves doing something or other. It was dwarves, so I didn't pay all that much attention."

"Well, anyway, it's true. The pipes go underground out to the point, mostly, and then they go way out to sea. Some dwarves told me."

"And you trust them?"

"Of course. Why wouldn't I?"

"Because… dwarves."

"Has any dwarf ever actually lied to you?"

"Yes."

"One you weren't trying to kill? Anyway, Weaver came up with the plan. Do you trust him?"

Rawk grunted and shoved his head back under the towel. "Don't you want to know where I'm going later?"

"No."

"I'm going to the Old Forest."

"Why?"

He cleared his throat. "The wolden wolf was wearing a collar."

"What?" a woman said from the doorway.

Rawk sat up so fast he almost fell over. He thought he might have pulled a muscle in his neck. He definitely hurt his knee. He cleared his throat.

"Hello, Melia." That was quicker than he had expected. He thought it wouldn't have been until the next day, at least.

"Hello, Rawk."

"Good to see you." Unlike Silver Lark, Melia looked older than she had twenty years ago, but she still looked good. Even now, it was obvious where Adalee had gotten her beauty.

Melia raised an eyebrow and Rawk cleared his throat again.

"Did I hear correctly?" she said.

Rawk didn't want to commit to any line of conversation. He could pretend her arrival was a coincidence. "Hear what?"

"Was the wolden wolf wearing a collar?"

That. Right. "Yes."

"Does Weaver know?"

"No. I don't see why he needs to."

"Because—"

Rawk waved away the words she hadn't yet spoken. "Yes, I know. But that doesn't mean I'm going to tell him anything. Let's change the subject."

She raised her eyebrow again. "Really?"

Rawk knew he'd made a mistake but it was too late now.

"You would rather we talk about Adalee?" Melia asked.

"No."

"You just couldn't help yourself, could you?"

"I didn't know who she was, Melia."

"Stay away from her."

"What would *your* mother have done twenty years ago if she'd found out?" Rawk entered dangerous territory.

Two raised eyebrows. "She's young enough to be your daughter."

Rawk scratched his nose. "I was actually worried..."

Melia laughed. It was the very thing that he had first noticed about her. It was the thing he remembered most. "Don't be ridiculous. Do you know how many daughters you have, by the way? How many sons? It could be dozens."

Travis cleared his throat. "I'll just come back later, Rawk." He slipped out the door.

"Grow up, Rawk. If Edwin finds out..."

"He'll probably be flattered."

"You obviously don't know Edwin. He'll come up here with half a dozen men and worry about the consequences later."

She started to leave.

"It was nice to see you again, Melia. We should—"

"Don't, Rawk."

Rawk shook his head. "So now everything I say is about trying to get a woman into bed?"

Melia stared at him for a moment. "Stay away," she said. "If you so much as look at Adalee again, Edwin will be the least of your problems. I will cut off your balls with a very dull knife before he even gets close." She left him there on his knees, towel draped over his head like a desert tribesman.

"Path. That went well." He probed at his neck, trying to see if the injury was serious.

$$-O-$$

People rarely went to the Old Forest. The Fermi said the forest was a strange and powerful place. Everything converged in there, they said. The past and future. North, south, east and west. This world and other worlds. Badgers and weasels as well, for all Rawk knew. The Fermi wailed all sorts of woe upon those who ventured within.

As he stood looking at the trees, shading his eyes against the early afternoon sun, he decided that they were at least partially right. North south, east and west did meet there, or close enough. Katamood occupied a narrow strip of land that linked two huge continents and the oceans on either side brought ships from all around the world. The markets of Katamood were filled with people from all over the world because it was the natural place to meet. He grunted. Weaver's canal might not be such a bad idea after all, if only it didn't look so horrible.

Rawk glanced over his shoulder. There were Guards at the top of Sparrow Tower, but they weren't paying him any attention. There was also a small crowd on the top of the ruined wall, come to watch the Hero pay tribute to his latest conquest, he suspected. They could believe whatever they wanted.

He looked at the place where the wolf had lain. The ground was dark with blood but the area still seemed so benign, as if nothing had happened there at all, as if a life and death struggle had not taken place. A magnificent creature, gone so quickly. All that remained was a story about a wolden wolf. Hardly fitting. Weaver was probably already arguing with his tailor about the fit of his new cloak and deciding what sort of clasp he should use.

Rawk made his way to the first of the trees and got down on his hands and knees. After a short search he found the collar. It was longer than he remembered. He could have worn it as a belt, if he liked studded red leather. Had the exot really been that big? That seemed impossible, and he'd stood face to face with it. And if the collar was big, the implications were even bigger. Who put the collar on it? And where were they now?

Rawk checked over his shoulder again and stepped into the shade. He stopped a few paces in. He drew his sword and gripped the collar tighter.

Some places are called old because they've been around a long time. Others are called old because they give the impression they've been around *forever*. They are deep and heavy in all the ways it is possible to be. The Old Forest was like that. He could feel the weight of the place on his shoulders. He could feel the weight of it in his lungs. And it took a moment, standing there with the sound of pumping blood loud in his ears, before he realized that the weight wasn't necessarily a bad thing. The weight on his shoulder could be a comforting hand as easily as it could be a yoke. Nothing there made him feel uneasy. It was merely the unknown eating at him. The unknown and the collar in his left hand. He shifted his grip on *Kult* and continued forward, following a wisp of a path that would probably disappear at any second and leave him lost like someone in a fairy story, comforting hand or not.

Brambles caught at his leg and he cursed. He hacked with his sword, wondering if he should just tell Lakin about the collar and be done with it. But Lakin would tell his commander and the commander would tell someone else and Weaver would get involved and all of a sudden it would be a big thing. Weaver would introduce a thousand new laws to make sure everything, and everyone, was under control. And he would send platoons of men into the Old Forest to investigate. Rawk felt the forest in his blood and knew he didn't want that to happen. Not until he was sure, at any rate. Not until he had a chance to kill the exot and claim the bounty for himself. It was too good an opportunity to hand over to Weaver.

He finally pulled his foot free and looked around. He ducked, and the club whistled over his head.

"Path!" Rawk wanted to back-pedal, but the briar was there, ready to trip him up. He scrambled away in the other direction.

The creature was as big as a house. Well, it seemed to be. A small house, admittedly. It was shaggy and grey and had shoes the size of water troughs. And the club was a small tree. Literally. It looked as if it had been freshly torn from the ground.

Rawk turned back and set himself, *Kult* at the ready. The sword might have been ready, but he wasn't. His hand was shaking. He wiggled his leg, trying to work out if his knee would behave. He wanted to wipe sweat from his face but wasn't willing to take the risk.

The exot gestured and it took a moment for Rawk to realize what it was referring to. He held up the collar, but apparently he should've hidden it.

The creature's eyes narrowed. "Where is Kaj?"

Rawk swallowed. "The dog is dead."

It charged forward and Rawk dived away. The tree-club hummed through the place he'd been standing. He found his feet and drew in a deep breath as he backed away a few more paces, trying to give himself time to think. He'd dropped the collar and the exot moved to pick it up.

Rawk watched. What would he have done twenty years ago?

Twenty years ago he would have run out onto the open ground so the audience, however small, could see.

After all, it was no use fighting a giant if nobody knew about it. But he was about twenty yards from the open ground and would never make it.

The giant stalked towards him.

The next time the club started to swing, Rawk dived towards his enemy. He hit the ground and rolled, swinging his sword. The keen edge bit into flesh near the knee and the creature wailed in agony.

Rawk pulled the sword free. Up on his feet, he grimaced as he limped two steps to the side. He attacked a hamstring and the creature cried out again, a very human sound that echoed around the forest. Rawk swung *Kult* for the third time and the sounds ended in a soft gurgle.

He stood and watched, not moving, until a slow steady drip of blood started to set his nerves on edge.

It wasn't his blood. So that was a good thing. Though the bandage on his arm reddened by the moment. Rawk sat in a patch of dirt and breathed. He quite liked it, even without the tea. He flexed his hand and looked at the growing stain of red on his bandage.

Rawk licked his lips.

The creature stared at him with one blank eye. A curtain of long, grey–white hair covered the other. It didn't look fierce now. It didn't look dangerous. Just sad. Sad and alone. There was a metal amulet and ribbons in the hair, red and green and yellow, and a tattoo on the one visible cheek. A bird of some kind, maybe. Impossible to tell for sure. It still clutched the collar in its huge hand.

"Now what?" he asked. The creature didn't answer. He looked back towards the city and, through a gap in the trees, saw several men racing across the open ground from Sparrow Tower. They slowed as they came closer, wary of whatever had made the noise, but they kept coming.

At least he wouldn't have to drag the damn giant out into the open.

Rawk sat quietly, taking deep breaths and waiting for the soldiers to arrive.

–O–

"That's not a wolden wolf either," Waydin said.

Rawk turned to look at him. There were ten other soldiers with him. "How can you tell?"

Waydin stared at the creature and didn't reply.

"Right. Well, I'll keep that in mind in the future. Now, seeing we've established that it isn't a wolden wolf, do you have any idea what it actually is?"

Waydin chewed on his lip for a moment, then shook his head. "Some type of troll maybe. But I'm not an expert."

"I'm somewhat of an expert, but I've never seen anything like." Rawk hauled himself to his feet with a grunt of effort.

"Are you all right?"

"Fine." He dusted himself off. "So, what do we do now?"

Waydin looked around, as if instructions might be written on a tree. "Not my problem. I'll tell someone, then do what I'm told."

"As ever."

"I think the dwarves all the way out in the lighthouse would have heard that scream."

"Well, you let me know how it goes, will you. I'm going home."

"That's it?"

"What do you want me to do? You can tell Lakin as well as I can."

"Yes, but they'll probably want to ask you some questions?"

"Like what?"

Waydin shrugged. "I don't know."

But he was probably right. *They* normally did have all sorts of questions. And *they* usually managed to turn up during lunch or dinner to ask them.

"They know where to find me."

Rawk trudged back across the open ground. The small crowd cheered as he came closer but their hearts weren't in it. They watched the forest, ready to run if any creatures emerged. If they were worried they should have been running already, at least putting a few more potential victims between themselves and the threat. But they were people, so they stood on the grass and on the tumbled down wall, cheering and keeping an eye out for more excitement. Rawk flexed his hands, returned greetings and shuffled towards the *Hero's Rest*.

He would sit in the taproom, drinking cool water and telling anyone who would listen about his bravery. That was a good way to spend the afternoon. He just had to get there first.

It was just like the good old days. Except he didn't remember them ever feeling like this.

At the base of the hill, Rawk came across one of the many little markets that dotted the area. He was half way along the street, smiling to the locals as he tried to negotiate the press, when he noticed a stall selling books. He slowed as he went past, trying to scan the titles. But the writing was too small to read, so he stopped and pretended to adjust his boot so he could lean in closer. Nothing that would help. He sighed and almost kept walking, so he could sit in the taproom of the *Hero's Rest* and drink some water and regale the customers with tales of the day's deeds. But his arm ached. And his knee and his back. And at his age if you stand still too long you fall over dead. And it was time to grow up, apparently.

So he tried to work out where the next of the city's markets might be and turned aside. He was just three blocks from the market they called Mount Cheese, after the two streets that met at the little square, when he came across a bookshop. The narrow building had a bright green, tiled roof and red plaster between the exposed frame of the wall.

Rawk stood across the road and wondered if he should continue to the markets instead. There was probably no right answer. Or, at least, none that he would find until he went into the shop to see if they had what he wanted. He straightened his torn shirt, winced at the flare of pain in his arm, and hurried across the street before someone saw him or he had a chance to change his mind.

He might have changed his mind anyway, halfway through the door, but a bell rattled and clanked with the movement and a stoop backed, red haired old man came from out the back.

"Hello, hello, hello," he said, blowing dust of a scroll case. "What can I..." When he looked up his eyes narrowed. "So, what can I do for you today, sir?"

Rawk cleared his throat. "I want to buy a book."

"Do you now? A particular book? Or will any do?"

"Not a *particular* book. But a book about a particular subject."

"So, even a scroll would do, at a pinch?" The old man smiled.

"I suppose it would, old man."

"My name is Juskin."

It still felt rude to not introduce himself. "Hello, Juskin, I'm—"

Juskin waved him away. "I have too many customers to remember all their names, my friend. You just buy your book—or scroll—" he smiled again, "and be on your way. I am sure to forget you were even here a moment after you leave."

Rawk gave a nod and decided he liked Juskin. "I would prefer a book, I think. Scrolls just seem to be waiting to be squashed or torn if you ask me."

"So, what would be the subject of this book?"

"Ahhh... Exots. Or ancient creatures. Or peoples. Or..." He cleared his throat again and looked around. There was nobody else in the shop. "I killed something today..."

"Oh, so not just any mythical, ancient peoples. But a *particular* mythical, ancient people."

"Yes."

"Hmmm..." He went around behind the counter and hauled himself up onto a stool. "You don't know the name of this creature by any chance? No, I thought not." He pulled a contraption of timber and glass from inside his robe and put it on his face. "That makes it decidedly more difficult, of course."

"And expensive, I imagine."

Juskin looked over the top of the thing on his face and drew himself up. Rawk held up a placating hand and the old man settled down again a moment later. "If you want haggling and tricks you've come to the wrong place."

Rawk gave a rueful smile. "I must admit that it isn't often I shop beyond the confines of the markets."

"That is true with most people, unfortunately. Do all your shopping in the one place. You may end up with bruised apples and books with missing pages, but they were cheap and you got home quicker, right?"

"Right. Look, I'm sorry, but what in Path's name do you have on your face?"

"They are called spectacles. I read about them in an old book that I found and had a dwarf make them for me. It took months to get everything right."

"And?"

"They help me see. Too much reading has effected my eyes, I'm afraid." Juskin pulled a book from under the counter and thumped it down, sending out a huge puff of dust. "Now, what did this creature look like?"

"Ten foot tall. Solid. Hairy."

"Two legs and two arms?"

"I said it was a person, didn't I?"

Juskin looked over the top of his spectacles again. "You think all 'people' look like us?"

"Well, don't they?"

"Three doors down is a hatter who was born with only one leg. And I know of a woman who has webbing between her fingers, like a duck."

"Yes but..."

"And horhars?"

"A horse with a human head?"

"What else?"

"They aren't real."

"Are you sure? Maybe they are not here today. But what of ten thousand years ago? Myths and legends normally start with a grain of truth."

"Yes, two arms and two legs. All where you would expect them to be."

"And hairy you say? Hairy like a hairy man? Or hairy like a bear?"

"Ummm... Like a bear, I think. Long, grey hair."

"Right." Juskin pushed his spectacles back up on his nose and started to leaf through his book.

"Is that a book of creatures?"

"Not details, no. This is an index of creatures that I have compiled. You look up attributes and get a list of candidates. So I look up 'hairy' and see the names. Then I look up 'ten feet tall' and see if any of them match." He spent several minutes reading and turning pages and mumbling to himself. "Here see, there are only two creatures that have those two attributes and one of them, the *gigapo* is described as willowy, not solid. The other, the Harien Troll, must be the one you are after. Or if not, I'm afraid I can't help you."

"Right, so have you got a book?"

Juskin pulled a second book from under the counter and started going through the pages. "I don't think... Ahhh, wait a moment." He disappeared back out through the door and for the next few minutes thumping and banging sounds emerged.

"Do you need help?" Rawk asked after an especially loud crack.

"No. No. I have it now." There was another bang, then silence. The silence stretched on for a few seconds and Rawk worried the old man had been trapped under a toppled mountain of books. But just as he was about to go to investigate, Juskin emerged carrying a small, leather bound volume. "Here we are."

He slapped it down on the counter and spun it to face Rawk.

"*Frento Magan's Compendium of Myth and Legend,*" Rawk read. "Sounds impressive."

"Doesn't it, though?" Juskin removed his spectacles and cleaned them on the corner of his robe. "Frento was a bit of a fool when it came to doing his own research, but he could edit the work of others like nobody else."

"And which is this?"

"His own work, unfortunately. And probably one of his poorer efforts as he was barely out of his teens when he did it."

"You knew him?"

"Oh, Path no. He lived about a thousand years ago. I may be old, but I'm not *that* old." Juskin laughed. "Now, are you going to have a look, or not?"

Rawk opened up the book and turned to the table of contents at the front. It ran for several pages, in very small, neat writing. He cleared his throat and held the book a little bit closer. Then a little bit further away.

Ruskin cleared his throat and offered Rawk the spectacles. "Do you want to try these?"

But his eyes were adjusting and he could see well enough. "No, thank you. I just..."

"Of course."

Rawk found the listing for Harien Trolls and leafed through the crackling pages until he found the right one. The first thing he saw was an illustration that took up a quarter of the page. It wasn't very good.

"Is that the one?"

"Yes... Well, it could be. Though I don't remember the legs being different sizes. And its head wasn't that lopsided."

"I imagine you can sometimes miss important details in the heat of battle."

"Obviously." Rawk said. "So, how much is the book?" There wasn't a lot of writing about the trolls. If he kept Juskin chatting long enough he could read it before he left the shop.

The old man looked him up and down. "For you, 100 ithel."

"100 ithel?"

"One of a kind book. Famous author."

"*Unreliable* author, I've heard."

"Illustrated. Look at that illumination."

"Is that a beetroot stain?"

"Perhaps. And that is most certainly tomato." Juskin smiled. "Oh, all right then. 80 ithel."

"I thought you didn't haggle."

"Who told you that?"

"You."

"Well, I thought you didn't read."

"Who told you that?" It was true. Heroes didn't read, except maps and street signs, perhaps. They killed and drank ale and did Heroic things. Reading wasn't Heroic. "80 ithel for the book," Rawk said, handing over the money. "And twenty ithel for the effort. And the discretion."

"You do drive a hard bargain."

Rawk slipped the book under his shirt and headed out the door, hoping nobody would see.

"Come again," Juskin called after him.

Out on the street, Rawk stopped to look. There was nobody in sight so he hurried away, as if just standing outside the shop would ruin his Heroic reputation. In a couple of minutes he reached the Mount Cheese Markets and was already being trailed by a group of half a dozen boys. He nodded and smiled to them and they pretended to be looking at a rack of flowing green dresses from Quera. Not really their style.

Right beside the well in the center of the small square, half in the shade of the dragon statue, a merchant sold inks, dyes, old whitewashed paper and scraps of cloth. And right up one end of the table was a small pile of books. Rawk pretended to look at the dyes while he scanned the titles, blinking as his eyes adjusted again. There was nothing there, just romances, so he nodded to the merchant and put down the bottle he'd been holding. The bottle itself was beautiful, but the dye was a horrid blue.

By the time Rawk made it to the other side of the square the boys had worked up the courage to talk to him. One second, they were hanging back, this time examining the melons in a fruit seller's barrow, and the next they were crowding around asking a dozen questions at a time. Finally, they slowed down and came to the general consensus that they wanted to hear a story.

It was a good excuse to sit and have a rest, if nothing else. "I battled a troll just an hour ago," Rawk said, sitting down on the edge of a porch. "It was—"

"No," said the biggest of the boys. "Tell us about the galangs?"

"The galangs?"

"Yes, the ones where you were hiding in the tree."

"The ones with Prince Weaver?"

"Yes."

"Well, all right then. I suppose." They obviously knew the story, so Rawk didn't know why they wanted to hear it again. Especially since it hadn't been all that interesting the first time. But he wasn't going to argue, so he tried to give the tale a new spin.

Five minutes later, the boys were howling with laughter as Weaver fell in the mud while searching for his dropped sword. That hadn't actually happened, but Rawk thought it a nice addition. And after the last of the creatures died he sent the boys on their way with a half ithel each.

Then he sighed and started the long, slow walk up the hill. At the top he looked at Weaver's palace. He knew he should go and report the troll but he turned the other way and headed for the *Hero's Rest*. He slogged up the stairs like he was climbing a mountain, then stopped just inside his room, leaning against the door. His arm throbbed. His head ached. His knee felt as if it was going to lock up at any moment and refuse to ever move again.

He wondered where he was supposed to sit. "Why don't I have a chair?" He didn't do much sitting in there, he was either in bed or heading out the door, but a chair still seemed like a sensible piece of furniture to have. It seemed like a grown–up piece of furniture to have. He sat on the bed and opened the Compendium.

"*Harien trolls are quite possibly the stupidest beings to ever aspire to being more than animals. They are angry and violent. They might well be warlike, if having wars didn't involve a measure of cooperation. They are more likely to kill their allies—they are closer after all—than the enemy and may well get bored of the whole thing and leave to find some easier prey. Distract them with shiny things or ply them with alcohol and all will be well.*"

Rawk laid back and stared at the ceiling. The book didn't tell him all that much at all. Ruskin had warned him, but he'd hoped anyway.

Harien trolls were big and mean. But he'd known that before he'd entered the shop. It didn't mention magic, but the one he'd killed had definitely looked like a shaman of some kind. And it had to make a ohoga portal. So, big and mean and knew something about magic. *Great. Not a lot of help if one of them comes to the city and starts clubbing people. Or spitting lightening at them.* He wondered if he should find a pen and add a notation to the book.

Sunday

THERE WAS A KNOCK at the door and Rawk jumped. "Yes."

The door opened and Mykle peered nervously around the edge. It must have been serious as he rarely left the common room.

"What is it?" Rawk asked.

"Weaver's here."

"Path. Is he in disguise?"

Mykle shook his head. "All the usual followers are with him."

" ?"

A nod. "He doesn't like you very much."

"He thinks I slept with his wife."

Mykle gave that some thought. "Did you?"

"Yes. But in my defense, it was about ten years ago. They weren't married at the time. Not quite. And he wasn't a general. He was just a little snot nosed.." Rawk sighed. "Give me a minute."

He was dressed, but not wearing any shoes. He looked around for his boots but could only find one, so he didn't worry and followed Mykle down to the common room in his bare feet. He didn't even get a chance to greet the Prince.

"What's this?" Weaver said, slapping him in the chest with some rolled up paper.

Rawk looked at it for a moment without taking it. "It looks like some paper."

Weaver kept holding it out, so Rawk eventually took it. When he looked closer, he still didn't know. It was two large, cheap looking sheets of paper covered in small, impossibly neat writing. He shook his head. "Sorry, I still don't know."

Weaver took the papers back from him and opened them out. He showed one to Rawk. There was a black and white sketch of the troll.

"Oh." Rawk read the writing that apparently went with the sketch. "*Rawk is one of the greats. He is perhaps* the greatest Hero to ever walk the world. But ever since Prince Weaver fought his final battle, against the sorcerers and the danger they bring to the world, Rawk's life has dramatically changed. There are no monsters for him to battle, no great deeds to be done.

"But a couple of days ago, that changed with the arrival of the first wolden wolf that has been seen in this area in more than a decade. It was a huge beast that many a lesser man, many a younger man, would have run from. But Rawk would not leave such a beast around to harass our great city and went out to meet it.

"Much of Katamood turned out to watch Rawk do battle. He prevailed, as he always has, as he always will, but not without taking injuries. He did not want the people of Katamood to worry, so he said nothing, but his wounds were so serious that he sought the assistance of a healer. And before his wounds had healed, he went out to the Old Forest again, looking to bring back the glory days of the Age of Heroes. And there, amongst the cold dark of the ancient forest he came across an even greater beast. The mighty troll towered above him, swinging a tree trunk as a club. There was a mighty battle.

"I saw this battle, hiding in the trees in fear of my life. I was ready to give aid, if required, but Rawk again prevailed, as he always has, as he always will. He slew the beast then paid it homage as men of the City Guard rushed to clean up the aftermath.

"Since then I have tried to discover the name of the conquered beast, but have found nothing. All I know is that I feel safe with Rawk walking the streets of Katamood."

"Well?" Weaver said.

"It was only a small tree."

"What?"

"It was—"

"I heard what you said, Rawk." Weaver sighed. "Why did you go back out there?"

"Out where?"

Weaver didn't say anything.

"To look."

"At what?"

"At where I killed the wolden wolf." Rawk looked around the room. Everyone was listening, but Weaver didn't take the hint.

"We both know that wasn't a wolden wolf, Rawk."

"It was according to this thing." He indicated the papers he still held.

"The people are calling it a newspaper. But stop changing the subject."

"I didn't change the subject. Nice weather we've been having."

"Why did you go back, Rawk? You've never been sentimental."

"I'm getting old."

Weaver just looked at him. Rawk turned to Ramaner for help but that was just crazy.

"All right. Well..." He looked around at the people in the taproom again and Weaver finally took notice.

"Let's step through here," the Prince said.

They went back out the door Rawk had entered by and stood at the bottom of the stairs. Ramaner went with them but the others, two Guards and a secretary, stayed where they were.

"Now, tell."

"The wolf was wearing a collar."

"And you knew about this three days ago?" Ramaner's jaw clenched. He was only about forty years old but already had the steely eyed stare perfected.

"Perhaps."

"And you didn't think to tell anyone?"

"I was injured, remember? I wasn't thinking straight, or something. I went to see a healer and she told me to go home and not do anything."

"So why didn't you?"

"When have I ever listened to a healer?"

"Well, you look fine to me. Even after fighting a troll."

"Janas is a good healer."

"Janas is dead, Rawk," Weaver said.

"Well, yes, I know but... Stop changing the subject, Weaver. There isn't anything anywhere that says I have to tell you anything at all. It's my job to kill exots and... whatever... not to tell *you* about the details. There's no law."

"Well, there damn well should be," Ramaner said.

Weaver sighed and held up a hand. "Rawk is right, Ramaner. He doesn't have to tell us anything if he doesn't want. Though, I'm sure if he thought there was an urgent need he would do so..."

"Of course I would. It was just one creature."

"Just one wolden wolf and a troll," Ramaner said. "That's two creatures. Two *exots*. And the fire thing. It says a lot that *that* didn't even rate a mention."

Weaver gave the man a cold look. "And what was the troll doing there, do you think?"

"Catching butterflies?" Rawk suggested.

Ramaner opened his mouth to say something. It was obviously going to be a loud and angry something.

"Well, how am I supposed to know? I went back to have a look and it attacked me."

Weaver held up a hand to stop Ramaner from talking again. "Is there anything to suggest there might be more of them?"

"No. I actually read about them in a book. It said they are solitary creatures, more likely to kill each other than actually cooperate."

Weaver nodded. "You can't be sure though, can you?"

"Not really."

"Any thoughts on how it got there?"

"It had ribbons in its hair, fetishes, that kind of thing, so I imagine it's a magician of some kind."

"Right, so if it was the magician there isn't necessarily another magician running around out there?"

"Exactly."

"Excellent then. Good. That's what I needed to hear." Ramaner started to say something but Weaver held up his hand without even looking. "Leave us for a moment, Ramaner."

"Your Highness?"

"Do you really thick Rawk is going to kill me? He would never do something like that, would you, Rawk?"

"Well, I must admit, the thought has crossed my mind at various times over the last forty years."

Ramaner grunted, gave Rawk a cold stare, then turned and headed back into the common room.

The door had barely closed behind him when Weaver started to talk. "What was it like?" He grabbed Rawk's shoulders. "Was it just like old times? Did you taunt it so it attacked or did it just attack?"

Rawk tried to get in a word or two though it didn't matter. Weaver would believe what he wanted anyway so it was best to let him go.

But finally, the Prince *did* stop. "Well?"

Rawk thought of telling his friend that it was nothing like old times. That he'd been scared. That he could've died. "Of course it was just like old times," he said. "It was just like the story said."

Weaver smiled, obviously reliving the battle in his mind. After a moment he gathered his thoughts. "I think I'll send someone to investigate the Old Forest anyway."

"Why?"

"There could be more. You *are* just guessing, after all."

Rawk gave a nod. "Can you let me know what you decide before you do anything?"

"Why would I do that? It's not my job to tell you anything at all."

"You're right. But do you want the people to panic? If you send off a troop of the Guard to go traipsing around the Old Forest, everyone will assume there's trouble, especially if this..."

"Newspaper?"

"Yes. Especially if the newspaper says something about it."

"Well, you started all the trouble"

"I didn't start anything. I just killed a wolden wolf."

"We both know it wasn't a wolden wolf."

"The newspaper says it was."

"And you believe it?"

"Don't see why I wouldn't."

Weaver grunted. "You might have a point. But I still don't think I'll tell you."

"Anyone can send in the army, Weaver. Where's the romance in that?"

It looked like Weaver was about to relent but, after a moment, he shook his head. Rawk couldn't say he blamed him.

"And when can I get my money, by the way?" Rawk asked. If he was going to annoy the prince, he might as well do it properly.

"What money?"

"*What money?* A hundred ithel for the wolden wolf. Though we both know that wasn't a wolden wolf," he smiled. "And that price is for ten years ago so it really should've increased. And a thousand for the troll."

"A thousand for the troll?"

"Large, sentient creature fighting with a weapon. One thousand ithel. Or are you saying it wasn't large?"

Weaver's lip twitched. "As you said, those contracts were from ten years ago. I think I could find several lawyers who will argue that they are invalid."

Rawk shrugged. "Fair enough. I'll just find out who makes this newspaper thing and I'll let them know what you said."

Weaver held up a hand. "All right. Give me a couple of days. Don't annoy me in the meantime." And he left before Rawk could get in the final word. At least, he left before Rawk could get in more words so Weaver would have to think of some new final words.

Rawk trudged back upstairs to his room, bare feet cold on the worn stones, and sat down on the bed. He closed his eyes and put his head back, wondering if he could go back in time a few days and hide somewhere before Waydin came to tell him about the wolden wolf. He could just forget the last few days and go back to complaining how there was nothing for a Hero to do.

Eventually, he sat up and looked around for his lost boot. He saw a leather toe sticking out from under the bed and stretched out to drag it into the open with his foot. But he had to get up any way, so he could go and get some clean, wool stockings from the drawer. As long as Travis had gotten them washed and put them away.

Rawk grunted. "Of course he has." He didn't know what Travis was being paid, but it probably wasn't enough.

Rawk started pulling the stockings on, but he paused when he noticed how dirty his feet were. And they stank. That happened when you kept them shoved in boots all day long, he supposed. But what was the use of spending money on clean clothes if they were dirty before he finished putting them on? He checked his arm. It was dirty too. And his armpit smelled as bad as his feet.

He was about to send for some water, but Travis wasn't working, so someone else would have to do it and Rawk didn't want to deal with someone else. And there was the room next door. With the shower. *Bloody dwarves. Again.*

Rawk left his stockings where they were and slipped behind the tapestry. He paused outside the door to the shower room again. He would much rather go through the next door. It had only been a couple of days since he'd exercised but he missed it already. *Nothing strenuous for a week. Bloody elves. When had he started listening to elves?* He ran his hand over his scalp and went into the shower room.

He stared at the shower. It didn't attack him. It didn't do anything sinister at all. Just some pipes and taps. And dwarves had built it. He tried to think if any dwarves *had* ever lied to him. He tried to think of one instance where they had done a poor job of whatever it was they were doing. He tried to think of one complaint about dwarves that related to their work and not their smell or the endless talking and singing or even to their very existence.

With a grunt, Rawk started stripping off his clothes.

There was a clean towel hanging on a hook and some soap on a plate on the floor.

He stepped under the water. It was cool, but he could feel the dust and grime washing away. The warm water was even more amazing than the cold water. He didn't know how it worked, but was glad that it did.

–O–

Scrubbed clean, Rawk got a fresh set of clothes and sat on the bed. He picked up the newspaper and read the story about the troll again. Then he had a look at some of the other stories. A dead man washed up near the docks. A wagon broke an axle halfway across a bridge upsetting traffic in the morning rush. An unknown dwarf was going around trying to sell faulty tools. And Adalee Dan Beketh had been seen coming down from the private rooms of the *Hero's Rest.*

Rawk swore. He reread the short, one paragraph story. He swore again. Melia had never been prone to exaggeration, as far as he knew, so if Edwin happened to have one of the newspapers... What was he supposed to do about that? He could possibly fight off Edwin and a couple of thugs, but he really didn't want to.

A few minutes later, still trying to come up with a solution, Rawk went down stairs with *Kult* at his hip. He paused in the doorway to the common room and looked around. There was no trouble, but that didn't mean it wouldn't turn up at any second. Instead of going to his usual seat, he slipped through the noise, waving and smiling when required, and headed out to the kitchen.

The breakfast crowd was in, so there were two cooks and three helpers filling the warm, smoke filled space. Kalesie worked at the main bench, slicing beef with a knife that was large enough to fight off grimkins.

Rawk snagged a helper, a boy barely into his teens who had once lived on a makeshift platform in the roof of the stables. Maybe he still lived there. "I want a plate of beef with potatoes and gravy please, Valen. I'll be over there."

"Yes, Rawk."

Rawk took a seat in a quiet corner and took out his knife and fork. Breakfast arrived a few minutes later and he ate silently, wondering what to do next. He flexed his arm, though he knew how it was going to feel. He didn't want to go out into the forest looking for another troll, not today, but opportunities for Heroic deeds were few and far between and without Heroic deeds he was no different to any of the veterans who sat around telling stories about the good old days.

Weaver wasn't going to tell him what was going on, but somebody else might...

When he finished eating he cleaned his knife and fork, slipped them into the belt pouch and made his way out the back door. He paid off two urchins at the gate and started down the hill. The barracks were about half a mile away. It was one of the few stone buildings in the city and one of the least impressive, despite its size. It was low and wide, but the stone was dirty and unfinished, as if it had come straight from the quarry. Rawk couldn't remember how long the building had been there, but he doubted

Weaver would have agreed to such an ugly place being built in his city. And, seeing it was so poorly constructed—there were gaps between stones that he could poke an entire finger into—it probably hadn't been done by dwarves.

There was a guard tower over the door with a man at the top. "Ho, Rawk. Have you come to join the Guard?"

Rawk shaded his eyes and looked up. "Not unless the pay has increased, Kenyon. And not as long as you're still here."

"Are we supposed to get paid?"

"So I hear. Is Waydin home?"

"Not a clue."

Someone poked their head out of the level below. "He's on Dung Patrol today."

"Dung Patrol?"

"He's cleaning the stables."

"And there's another reason to not join the Guard."

Kenyon signaled to someone else and a small door set into the larger, iron–banded main door opened. Rawk stepped through and headed for the stables.

He found Waydin and five other men right where they were supposed to be, in the stables with shovels, barrows and rakes. But none of the tools were being used and the men were lazing around on the admittedly–clean, floor. They all jumped to their feet when he entered, before realizing who it was and sinking back down again.

"This sounded like a terrible duty," Rawk said. "Apparently I was wrong."

Waydin shrugged. "You can take all day to do it, or you can get it done quickly and take some time to relax. I've always been a fan of the latter."

"What happens if you get caught sitting around?"

Waydin snapped a salute from the ground. "We just this moment finished, sir, and were just taking a minute to rest before we went to see what else we can do."

Rawk raised an eyebrow. Waydin shrugged again.

"It's not often officers come in here. They send someone along to get their horse and meet them at the gate."

"It smells too much in here," one of the others offered.

"And it does," Rawk agreed. "So can we step outside for a minute, Waydin?"

Outside Waydin offered Rawk his flask of water. "What can I do for you?"

"I think Weaver is going to send someone into the forest to see if there are any more troll things."

"He'd have to, really."

"Right. But I want to get the trolls. It may be years before another chance like this comes along."

"So? Go and get them then."

Rawk held up his injured arm. "This really needs time to heal. Janas said—"

"I thought she died."

"Yes, look. I need to rest it as much as possible."

"So... You want me to dress up as you and go find the trolls?"

"Yes. That's exactly what I was thinking." Rawk sighed. "I need you to tell me what he decides to do. And more importantly, when he decides to do it."

"You want me to spy on Prince Weaver for you?"

"No, I want you to spy on the Guards so you can tell me what's being organized."

"Right. That's completely different, I suppose." He gave a nod. "I can't guarantee anything, but I'll see what I can do."

"Thanks, Waydin. I'll expect to hear from you in the next couple of days then."

"I expect so. Now let me get back to work."

"Of course. I wouldn't want to keep you from your duties." Rawk slapped him on the back and headed the other way. Next, he needed to work out what he was going to do about Edwin Dan Beketh.

–O–

When he heard footsteps on the landing outside, Rawk looked up from the book. He'd been sitting there for the last half an hour, trying to twist out more information while the afternoon shadows gathered in the corners. He'd read the passage a dozen times, and it still didn't tell him much at all. He couldn't imagine getting one of the creatures to drink alcohol. Did he offer it a tankard? Or perhaps he could just roll an entire keg towards it and hope it would know how it worked.

There was a knock at the door.

"Come in, Travis." Rawk rubbed at his aching eyes.

Travis opened the door and stood in the doorway. "That's a book."

Rawk looked down at the *Compendium of Myth and Legend*. "A book?" he said, sounding shocked and throwing it on the bed as if it was a hot coal. "Really? The merchant told me it was called a nariv."

Travis shook his head. "Nariv is fermi for book."

"I know it is, Travis."

"Right. Sorry. Anyway, I brought some hot water."

"Thank you."

They went through the routine, Travis working in silence. When the poultice was on his arm, Rawk place the towel over his head and breathed the fumes. He didn't mention the troll. The story would be all around the city by now so if Travis wanted to know, he could ask.

Travis cleared his throat. "I thought you might like to come to the Veterans' Club."

"I'm not a veteran." He knew he wasn't going to get out of it that easily.

"But you'll be my guest."

Rawk pushed away the towel and sat up. "And why would I want to go, exactly, when I can sit in the tap room here for much less effort? I have my new book to read."

Travis smiled and shrugged. "There's a play on. A tragedy. I thought you might like to see it."

"A play?" Rawk raised an eyebrow. "You want me to see a play?" He'd never seen a play in his life, apart from the type in the market place that he walked past without noticing.

"Why not, Rawk? Lots of people do it. It's at the Veterans' Club, so obviously lots of veterans do. It's not just for old ladies."

"A tragedy, you say?"

"Yes. There will be fighting and death and doom and all that kind of thing, I imagine."

"Are you supposed to be working tonight?"

"No."

"Then why are you here?"

"To ask if you want to go to the Veterans Club."

"Now?"

"Yes."

Rawk looked at the book and that decided it. "Oh, all right." He held out his arm to be bandaged.

Five minutes later they were walking down the long spine of the hill towards the river. The wind came from the east, bringing the usual smells of the sea and the wharves, like salty, week-old stew.

"So, Weaver hasn't come asking about the troll?" Travis asked.

"Of course."

"Why didn't you tell me? I would've come to watch."

"Most of the common room was watching for a while. Natan can probably give you the details."

"And I'm sure his version of events would be much more exciting than yours."

"Probably."

"It's a shame, really."

Rawk was a bit confused. "A shame that Natan doesn't let the facts spoil a good story?"

"No, that." Travis had stopped to look at the decaying facade of the Tapalar mansion.

Rawk looked too. "I suppose."

The small garden separating it from the road had once been full of topiaries and flowers and pristine lawn. Now it wasn't much more than a wild jungle. The front door was protected by a portico but still looked ready to fall apart. The bench to the left already had and several windows were letting the weather in through broken panes. The rail had come away from a small balcony up above and at least one grotesque had committed suicide by leaping down from the roof.

"It's been neglected ever since Lady Tapalar died," Travis said.

"It was never that nice inside."

"It's got great views, I hear. You can see the river and the bay from the back porch. Wait, how do you know what it looked like inside?"

"After her husband died, Lady Tapalar liked to invite all her friends around and have me tell them tales of daring and..." He waved his hand, "You know, stuff."

"Bravery? Heroism? Bullshit?"

Rawk gave a little smile as he continued to look at the house. "Pretty much."

"I heard she was a bit strange."

"Strange? I suppose. She would've been out there killing monsters herself if noble widows were allowed to do that kind of thing." Rawk gave a grunt of laughter. "I would've almost felt sorry for the monsters."

"I thought she was an old lady."

"Path, no. She was only a couple of years older than me."

Travis continued to examine the house. "It's got to be worth a fortune. And it's been sitting empty for ten years."

"Eighteen. She died eighteen years ago. Come on, let's go see some tragedy."

"Some *other* tragedy." Travis had one last look at the house before continuing on.

There was a group of men coming up the hill. Rawk examined each of the men in turn. None of them was Edwin Dan Beketh, but maybe he wasn't the type to come along to witness the dirty work, no matter what Melia thought. Rawk flexed his shoulder. His hand rested on the hilt of his sword but the men passed by without incident. He released a breath he didn't realize he'd been holding.

–O–

The Veterans' Club sat on a side street further down the the hill. It was an impressive full–timber building with a tower over the door and the ghosts of heraldry barely visible on the first story. Rawk paused outside the large, iron bound door.

"There's nothing to worry about. We're allowed to have guests."

"I'm not worried." Rawk followed Travis into a small foyer with a couple of open doorways in the back corners and another large door leading out the rear wall. A tall, muscular man stood in the middle of the room. Somehow he managed to look good in his embroidered finery. It was green and gold and red and could easily have looked ridiculous on another person.

"Hello, Barin," Travis said, smiling. "This is—"

"I know who it is, Travis," Barin said with a grunt. His voice was surprisingly soft. "Pleasure to have you with us tonight, Rawk."

"Nice to be here, I guess. Just coming to see the play, apparently."

"Play? We—"

"I think we're already a bit late, Barin," Travis said, slapping the other man on the back. "Probably shouldn't stand around chatting."

Barin paused for a moment, looking uncertain, then nodded and went to open the big doors behind him.

In the next room, Rawk stopped. It had once been an open courtyard, surrounded by two story buildings on all sides, but at some point a vaulted ceiling had been added to make a huge theatre. There were a couple of hundred chairs facing a large stage, plus more on balconies around the side.

"Impressive, isn't it?" Travis said.

Rawk nodded.

About forty people were watching as three men, dressed as women, screeched and threatened each other with pots and pans.

"So that's the tragedy is it? Not quite what I expected."

The crowd laughed as one of the 'women' fell off the stage.

Rawk grunted. "Well, I suppose they *are* fighting." But, *really* not what he expected.

Travis shook his head, confused. "That isn't a tragedy. I'm not sure what's going on. Faramon said—"

"Faramon? And you believed him?"

"All right, maybe he isn't the most reliable source of information but..."

The players on the stage were still screeching.

"I refuse to watch... *that.*"

"And I wouldn't expect you to. So, lets go see what's on in the Armory instead."

"The Armory?"

"Yes." Travis started to lead the way, around the outside of the chairs towards a door on the far side. "This place used to be the barracks, back when Katamood was barely a city and didn't need much protecting. Now, there's a taproom in the main bunk room, an eatery in the old mess hall, and a smoking room in the officer's board room."

"A smoking room?"

"Well, you don't have to smoke in there, obviously. It's just a quite place to sit, if you want. There's also some gambling rooms and a doctor and a banker and lots of things like that to support the veterans."

"Sounds like something Weaver would come up with."

"Well, he didn't. Something similar has been in Katamood since before any of us were born. It's just that it's grown a lot since Weaver came and turned Katamood into a place that normal people actually like."

Through the door they followed a short passage and made their way down some worn stairs. The Armory was low roofed and dimly lit. Brick columns around the walls created deep shadows that somehow avoided all the efforts of the lamps. There were tables and chairs and a bar over to the side. And up the front was a low stage. Nobody was on it yet.

"Nothing happening, by the looks of it," Rawk said.

"The lamps are lit, so someone will be on stage soon, I imagine."

"Oh, right."

"You sit down while I get some drinks. Do you want anything to eat?"

"No."

Rawk found a table at the back and lowered himself into the chair. There were a few others in the room, nursing drinks or finishing up a meal. Nobody paid him any attention.

"Here we go." Travis set a mug down in front of him and took a seat.

"How much was it?"

"I'm paying tonight."

"Is this a date, Travis?"

Travis laughed. "You wish, big fella. Can't a friend buy you a drink occasionally?"

Rawk stopped, mug half way to his mouth. "We're friends?"

"What else would you call it?"

"Well..." Rawk grunted. "I suppose."

Travis looked offended and Rawk held up a hand.

"It isn't that I don't like you, Travis, I've just never thought about it." He'd never really had friends before, unless you counted Weaver. Travis had run the *Hero's Rest* for more than five years and gone above and beyond the call of duty in a lot of areas, helping with things that weren't a part of the job. Rawk smiled and raised his mug. Is that what friendship was? Is that what it felt like? He gave a smile. "Well, here's to friendship, I guess."

Rawk downed some drink and nearly choked.

"Are you all right?"

He coughed and spluttered. "Fine. But it's water. I was expecting ale." He looked over to the bar to see if anyone was watching.

Travis shook his head and sighed. "Don't worry, I said it was for me. I told them a healer had told me I could only drink water for a week."

"Oh. Right then." He sat back, wiping water from his chin. "So when is this show going to start?"

But just then, two people walked onto the stage. The woman was small, with dark skin and hair. She wore a nervous smile and carried a mandolin. The other was a dwarf with a flat, handheld drum.

"A fermi and a dwarf?" Rawk said. "I won't..." He rose to his feet.

"Oh, sit down, Rawk."

"You knew about this? You didn't talk to Faramon at all, did you?"

"No, I didn't. This is the show I came to the other night." He looked up at the stage. "They're amazing and I thought you'd like it."

"Why would you think that?"

Travis laughed. "You can sit stonily at the back of the taproom all you like, Rawk, but it's obvious how much you like music. I don't know why a Hero isn't allowed to like music, by the way. Is a Hero not allowed to have fun? Are they not allowed to be people?"

"Well, a Garalon fiddler is quite different to... to this."

"Yes, it is. Because this is wonderful. This is like an ocean compared to your Garalon fiddler's muddy puddle."

"I doubt that very much." He was still standing with Travis' hand on his arm.

"Sit down, Rawk."

"I will not—"

"As a favor. For a friend. We can leave after the first song, if you want."

Rawk continued to stare at the pair on the stage. "This is why I don't have friends," he said when he eventually sat down.

"Yes. Because you're stubborn and difficult and don't know how to relax."

"That isn't what I meant."

"I know what you meant, now shut up."

Up on the stage, the dwarf had pulled up a little stool and started to play his drum, striking it with a double–ended stick.

Rawk had never heard anything like it. When he thought of drums he thought of the snare drums or the bass drums played by the military. Or perhaps the war drums of the northern plains. This was... different. Light and lyrical, with the soft echo of the room adding a chorus to the background. And then the woman played a stream of mandolin over the top, and Rawk could have listened all night. He stared. The audience was silent. They ignored their drinks and their food and their companions.

The music swept around the room for several minutes before the woman began to sing. Rawk started to rise, though he didn't know where he was going, then sank back to his seat. Her voice was soft and smooth, clinging to the notes around it like snowflakes in the breeze. He sat through three songs before he looked around again.

"Who is she?" he whispered into the bubbling silence between songs.

"Her name is Celeste. The dwarf is Grint. He's her brother, I think."

"What?"

"Yeah. Her father's a dwarf or something. But she looks more like her mother, obviously."

Rawk couldn't believe it. "How can a fermi–dwarf bastard sound like that?"

"Have you heard the dwarves sing?"

"Of course, they never bloody stop."

"Yes, but have you *listened?* Every one of them can sing. I have yet to meet a dwarf that couldn't."

"They just sing those work songs."

"When they're working, yes. And they do it well. I imagine they sing other songs after hours. The fermi aren't terrible either, though nothing like dwarves."

The pair on stage were playing again, so Rawk shushed his companion and turned to listen. This time, Grint sang as well.

Munday

THE OFFICES OF *KEETO ALATA* were on the mezzanine floor of a huge building down by the river. Rawk had seen the outside of the building often enough, but had never had reason to venture beyond the door. Climbing the stairs he looked out over the low wall to the warehouse down below. Most of the floor space was taken up by rolls of brocaded silk, though there were bales of something else piled almost to the ceiling in the back corner and also a couple of dozen timber crates. A few dwarves were loading a wagon, working by hand. It was obviously hard work, but they chatted amongst themselves, joking and laughing. The thick, throat–clogging scent of wheat filled the air.

Rawk continued across the large, open office. He smiled when the receptionist looked up. The young man's eyes went wide then stood up so quickly he knocked his chair over. He quickly righted it but apparently didn't use the time to work out what he was going to say. "Ahhh..."

Rawk held up a hand. "Hello. I'm Rawk."

"I know who you are."

Rawk sighed. "That's excellent." He waited a moment. "Now would be the perfect time for you to tell me who *you* are."

"Oh, yes."

"So?"

"I'm Hurno."

"A pleasure to meet you, Hurno." Rawk smiled but it didn't put the other man at ease. "I was hoping to speak with Yardi, if I could."

Hurno looked over his shoulder at the closed door. "Yardi is doing accounts this morning. She asked not to be disturbed."

"Well, could you disturb her just for a moment, to see if she will talk with me."

Hurno looked unsure. "I really don't think I should. Somebody made a mistake with the books and—"

Rawk called out. "Yardi!"

Nothing.

He tried again and a minute later the woman in question came through the door. She looked surprised.

"Rawk?" She was as thin as a Queran beggar, though she ate more than a party of Heroes.

"Yardi. Hurno said you were busy but I thought you might talk to me anyway."

"Of course. Hurno, this Rawk. He last great Hero, a giant among men. You not make giants wait."

Rawk smiled. Yardi spoke at least four languages and, though she generally got the words right, she often switched grammar and syntax mid sentence. It was amazing how such an intelligent woman could sometimes sound so silly.

Hurno looked flustered. "Sorry, I—"

"It does not mind. Come Rawk. I have been working on the books since before the dawning so somewhat of a distraction is welcome."

"What's the problem?"

"Somebody seems to have mislaid a few thousands ithel worth of sugar cane."

Rawk closed the door behind him and looked around the office. It was sparsely furnished with just one behemoth of a desk in the middle of the floor, three chairs, and a cabinet to one side. There was a door in the back wall that probably led to the mess. There was also a jungle of potted plants, lining the walls and hanging in baskets from the ceiling.

Yardi saw him looking. "They help me to relax."

"Really? Do you have to employ someone to keep them alive?"

The woman shook he head. "I manage all of that. It gives me time to think."

"Right." Rawk was doubtful. He liked plants well enough, but had never really considered having them inside.

"So, to what do I owe the pleasure? It a long time been."

"What do you know about Edwin Dan Beketh?"

She shrugged her bony shoulders. "Not a muchness. He arrived here from Tharpin when he was just a boy and started working as a runner for Gagan Fen. He ended up managing some operations before striking out on his own. Most everyone knows that. He is not one of the richest men in Katamood, but I believe that is mainly because he has a plethora of interests outside his businesses. He likes to enjoy life and not waste it working. And... he is tendering for the Melaworth contract."

Rawk shook his head. "I don't know what that is."

"The details matter not." She waved the details away. "The contract is worth muchness, that is all you need to know."

"Is he close to getting it?"

Rawk grew nervous as Yardi stared at him for a moment. "He is in the top two or three." She blinked slowly. "There are a few more things we need to be checking."

"So it wouldn't be a huge tragedy if he got the contract?"

Yardi's nose twitched. "If I remember correctly, you were not going to be coming in here asking for favors."

"I didn't ask for a favor. I just asked a question."

There was a long stretch of silence. "From what I have seen, it would not be a tragedy."

Rawk nodded. "Right. Yardi, I need a favor."

Yardi sighed and slumped back in her chair. "What is it all about?"

"I'm getting old, Yardi."

Her eyes narrowed. "This is news? We are all getting old."

"I know but... I'm starting to think that nothing is as it used to be."

"Again..."

"I can remember when husbands used to come after me. And paramours. Now I'm being chased by fathers."

Rawk looked up when Yardi burst out laughing. "You tumbled with Adalee Dan Beketh? Oh, Rawk, when will learn?"

"I think the day is fast approaching. And thank you for your support, by the way. Melia has already threatened me with castration."

Yardi tried to say something but it was lost amidst a fresh burst of laughter. Rawk sat in silence and waited for her to calm down. It took a while.

"So, can you give him the contract?"

"I really should deny you, just to be watching the fun."

"You'd enjoy that, wouldn't you?"

"Of course. But Edwin can have the contract, I suppose. I'll announce it in about a week."

"Thank you, Yardi."

"What are old friends for, Rawk?"

"Are we still friends? I mean, these days we hardly see each other and when we do we talk business."

"If friendship was about how much time you spent with someone, Hurno out there would be my best friend. Luckily, it's about what you would do for each other. So, you can make up your own mind."

"Where do you think we would be now, if I hadn't gone away?"

"Married, I dare say."

Rawk nodded. "Married and miserable."

"I would be miserable. You would be deliriously happy."

"Sorry, yes, that's what I meant." He smiled. "Deliriously happy and working for you on the docks back in Fabez."

Yardi was suddenly serious. "I think we would have driven each other crazy very quickly, Rawk."

"I can see that now," he agreed, "but at the time..."

"I know. I would have said yes in an instant."

They sat in silence until someone knocked on the door.

Yardi cleared her throat. "Yes, Hurno?"

The young man stuck his head in. "The chancellor is here."

"She's early."

"I know."

"I'll be out in a moment."

The door closed again.

"Slip out back if like."

"Will Huron tell?"

"He knows better than."

"Good. Are we friends, Yardi? Or is this something else?"

Yardi thought for a moment. "Yes, we are friends. It's complicated, but we are friends."

"Thank you." Rawk slipped out through the room's other door.

–O–

Rawk put the dagger back onto the cloth and picked up another, longer weapon and tilted it to catch the light.

"That is genuine redami steel."

Rawk didn't say anything. He tapped the dagger on the side of the wagon.

"And that is a ruby from the mines of Frensch."

"You think I'd buy a dagger because of a ruby on the hilt?"

"Well..."

"You think I'm some lord who wears weapons for show?"

"Of course not, Rawk. I was just—"

"The tang is broken," Rawk said. He tossed it down onto the cloth.

"I'm sure it isn't."

But Rawk had already wandered away. The markets were buzzing with activity. Five ships had berthed in the harbor that morning, disgorging an array of cargoes and hordes of foreign sailors with coin to spend. They moved around the stalls, chattering in their own languages and stuttering through half sentences with the locals. They shopped with abandon, seeming to want some of everything. A tall, bearded man bought a whole carton full of sweets. Another, no bigger than a dwarf, handed over fifty ithel for rolls of bright, colorful silk. He lugged them away, one on each shoulder. A woman, with blue and red hair and five rings in her ear, haggled to the last ithel over a carved wooden figurine. And wherever they went, the merchants worked harder to find sales amongst the locals as well.

One huge sailor, tattooed and hairless, swaggered over to a tent where another big man sat at a table.

"This will be interesting," Rawk muttered.

Hubb had been making a living from arm-wrestling for at least five years. He sat in his seat at various markets and people came and handed over their money. He did lose, but not often.

The sailor pulled out some coins, thumped them down on the table and sat down in the second chair. He stretched his arm, loosened his wrist and got ready. Hubb had been wrestling for most of the morning and was more than ready. It was all over very quickly. It always surprised Rawk how it took just a second for many strong men to lose. He'd come to the conclusion, long ago, that it was as much to do with technique as strength.

Rawk found a seat by the side of the river, watching as the crowd swirled past. Hubb took money off two more men who should have known better then stood up, stretched, and made his way towards Rawk.

"Anyone would think you've retired, Rawk. Sitting around here sunning yourself."

"Someone is looking for me so I thought I'd sit around in a public place for a while."

"Do you want Dan Beketh to find you or do you want enough witnesses that he'll have second thoughts?"

"You know about that?"

"Everyone does."

"Well, let's just pretend I want an audience," Rawk said. Then he changed the subject. "I thought you retired."

"I did." Hubb sat down and stretched his legs out before him.

"Did you run out of money?"

"I just spent so much time telling people I wasn't wrestling any more that I might as well have been doing it." He scratched the back of his hand. "It was like every time I walked into a room someone saw it as a challenge."

Rawk grunted. "I know what you mean."

"Wolden wolves following you around looking for a fight?"

"No. It's just, you know, expectations."

"Yeah, I know what you mean."

"You could come back and do Hero stuff again."

Hubb laughed. "Not on your life. I'm too old for that stuff now."

"Do you miss it though?"

He sat back. "Sometimes. Not so much though. Times change. We change."

"Perhaps." Rawk hadn't changed. He was starting to think he was the only one. These days the main part of his work involved walking around waiting for work and letting people marvel at how marvelous he used to be. He wondered why he *didn't* buy weapons for show.

After a couple of minutes talking, Hubb sighed and rose to his feet. "Back to it, I suppose. I think that guy over there is waiting for me." He sauntered back to his table leaving Rawk on his own.

Not far away, five dwarves were working at a bronze statue. It had been tilting further and further for the last few years but the dwarves had straightened it out and were now scrubbing rust from the metal. They worked with huge brushes and leather gloves that protected their hands from the acid they were using.

One of the dwarves saw Rawk and doffed his hat. "Mornin' to you, sir," he said.

Rawk grunted.

"Just need to finish cleaning this and we'll be out of your way."

"You aren't in my way," he replied.

"Right you are, sir."

"But that acid is hurting my eyes."

"Just a moment more of that."

"It's always just a moment more. A minute more. A day more. Can't you dwarves ever just be done with something?"

"We're done with that statue over there, sir."

Rawk looked. Another statue, not far away, that had been polished very recently. There was a crow on top, having trouble gripping as it tore at a piece of bread.

"And we're done with the uneven cobbles by the fountain. An old lady tripped on them yesterday and gashed her knee."

"Yes, but—"

"There's always more work to be done and never enough people to do it."

"Unless you're a Hero."

"Pardon, sir?"

"Never mind. Just finish the work and leave me in peace."

"We never stopped, sir, we never stopped."

And he was right. After his initial greeting, the dwarf had started to scrub again and hadn't let up since, as if making up for the five seconds he had wasted. The others had not even slowed.

Rawk was about to move on when a shadow fell across his position.

"Good morning, Rawk."

"Waydin. Are you following me?"

"That would be stupid. You know my face too well."

"I was just thinking that myself."

"We have other people for that." Waydin smiled but Rawk looked around, wondering.

"Are you sure nobody is following *you*?"

"I have a cover story."

"Out with it then."

"Weaver's sending Hawk Squad into the Old Forest to look for more of your trolls."

"Hawk squad?" He was taking it seriously then. "When?"

"Tomorrow morning. Do I get paid for this spying?"

"I'll organize something for you."

"Thanks. Also, I've been sent to let you know that today's lunch is at the *Mermaid's Tail*."

"Really? Today?" And, even worse, it was a sailors' tavern. Even the steak would taste like fish.

"Codename Besh. He's a sailor that came in on one of those ships today."

"Of course he is. So, wait a minute, you're getting paid to walk down here by me *and* by Weaver? Good work if you can get it."

"You didn't recruit me as your spy because I'm stupid."

Rawk grunted and watched as Waydin walked away. They weren't going to find any more of the trolls. The book was pretty clear; they wouldn't stand near each other long enough to all get through a portal. "That's no reason to let Hawk Squad take all the glory." He flexed his arm, wincing at the pain.

But before he even worried about trolls, he had to make it through lunch.

–O–

The *Mermaid's Tail* was a squalid little place right on the edge of the river. How it continued to occupy such prime real estate was beyond Rawk. And why Weaver would want to go anywhere near it was even more mystifying.

Rawk was early. He stood in the door for a moment, taking in the stench, and decided he would wait out on the porch. He sat down and the bare–footed old man on the next stool gave a small nod of greeting. Then the two of them sat in companionable silence for a while.

"You don't 'member me, do you?"

Rawk turned to look. "Should I?"

The old man took his pipe out of his mouth and tapped it on his hand before examining the bowl. "Up to Falangoon, about twe'ny fie years ago. You were after a sky–drake and—"

"And you got it before me. Of course I remember. How could I forget?" Rawk sat back and leaned against the wall. "Pick Karden."

The old man smiled. "Tha's me. Tha's me all right."

"I didn't know you lived down this way."

"Been here about fie years now."

Rawk wondered if 'here' meant on the porch of the *Mermaid's Tail.* "How long you been out of the business?"

"How long? You kidding? Quit not long a'er we met. Was too ol' even then, I reckon."

Rawk grunted. "How come, all of a sudden, everyone's telling me I should retire?"

Pick looked at him. "Ne'er said nothing."

"Maybe not, but you suggested it. How old are you?"

"Now?" He grunted and pulled on his long white beard. "Reckon I seen sisty–fie summers."

Sixty–five? He was ten years older than Rawk but he looked ancient. "So you were too old at forty?"

Pick shrugged. "You and me is diff'rent people. And times is different. It ain't like it used to be."

It was Rawk's turn to grunt. "So you're saying if there were any real monsters left to fight I would've quit years ago?" He wondered if that was the case. If he had to go out fighting harien trolls every week would he do it? Or would he be sunning his toes on the porch of some seedy tavern, waiting to tell a tale or two?

Pick pointed down the street. "Well, was nice ca'ching up."

Three 'sailors' were making their way towards the tavern. The outer two men of the little group walked like soldiers. The man in the middle walked like someone who'd once heard a description of how sailors walked and had then decided to try walking like the saltiest sailor who'd ever walked.

Rawk sighed and shook his head. "It certainly isn't like it used to be."

Pick laughed.

"Besh," Rawk called as Weaver got a bit closer. He rose to his feet and waved. "Never thought I'd see you around these parts. Not after last time."

Weaver looked stunned.

"Did you visit the whore again or think better of it?" Rawk didn't normally go in for the whole undercover thing at all, doing only what was necessary, but it was worth it this time just to see the look on the prince's face.

"Ahhh, Rawk." He straightened his cap. Rawk could see him thinking furiously. "No, I haven't seen her. And I'd appreciate it if you didn't tell her I was here." He was so flustered he didn't even think to use his terrible accent until half way through the sentence.

Rawk smiled some more. "Can I buy you and your friends a drink?"

"Of course you can. You can buy us lunch as well."

"Come on then."

Rawk paused in the doorway, hand on the hilt of his sword, silhouetted against the noon light. He pretended to look for a seat, but in reality he was blinking away tears as the fumes washed over him again. He coughed and stumbled inside, assuming Weaver would have organized a vacant table down the back somewhere. The taproom wasn't all that large but half the city seemed to be crammed in there. Rawk squeezed between the tables. He knocked off a man's klemper hat with his elbow and couldn't retrieve it because he couldn't find enough room to bend down. He apologized as he continued deeper into the madness.

There was a small island of calm down the back of the room. One table guarded by two hard eyed men who probably hadn't ever set foot on a ship in their lives. When they saw Rawk they downed the last of their drinks and rose to their feet and moved to stand nearby as if giving up the table was all very reasonable.

Rawk gave them a nod and sat himself down. Weaver joined him a moment later as his two companions took up positions on the other side.

"You couldn't find somewhere quieter, Besh?" Rawk asked as he sat down.

"I like it."

"Really?" Rawk doubted the owner of the *Mermaid's Tail* liked the place very much. "What's that smell?"

"All right, I've never been here. I picked it at random."

"It's a bloody sailors' tavern, Besh."

"How was I to know?"

"It's called the *Mermaid's Tail* and it's right beside the wharves."

"Well, yes. Obviously. But there are sailors' taverns and there are *sailors' taverns*."

"Well, next time don't pick either of them; I don't care how many ships have come in. Farmers are nice sensible people and there always lots of them around Katamood. Even merchants, for Path's sake."

"All right. Enough. So what are you going to eat?"

Rawk sighed. "I'll just have some fish."

"What sort?"

"Cooked, preferably. They all taste the same to me."

Weaver shook his head, but raised his hand to get the attention of a server. That was never going to work, so after a moment he called one of his minders and sent the man to find food.

Rawk sat back while he waited.

"I've been thinking about our conversation the other day," Weaver said.

"Which one?"

"About going back to the old days. I thought I could take a vacation."

"You want to take a vacation?" Rawk raised an eyebrow.

"Yes. The two of us could get on a ship and go somewhere I won't be recognized. We could go somewhere far from here and find some exots to kill."

Rawk laughed before he realized Weaver was serious. "You're kidding. First of all, it would probably take us a week to get far enough to be guaranteed to find anything to kill. And even then, it might take us a week to find anything. Then a week to get back, if you haven't gone and done something like lose your arm."

"So?"

"So you want to leave Katamood for three weeks, minimum? You want to put some flunky in charge while there are trolls and fire sprites and wolden wolves all over the place?"

Weaver rubbed the tip of a finger on the greasy table–top. "That wasn't a wolden wolf."

Rawk sighed. "And your bloody canal is almost done."

"But think of the stories we could tell, Rawk. Battling ferocious beasts. Camping out under the stars. Just the two of us and a camp fire."

"And mosquitoes. And leeches. The thing about the old times is that they are always good. We joke about sleeping under trees and stealing eggs and whatever else as if we would do it all again if it meant having the battles and the camaraderie again."

"And the sex."

"But we don't mention the sleeping in mud and standing in chicken shit in our tales, except as a bit of comic relief, because the public doesn't want to know about it. And I don't either, Weaver."

"But—"

Rawk held up a hand. "Everyone keeps telling me I should grow up, even old Pick out on the porch, but I already have. This is a grown up version of a Hero. I don't need to sleep in barns, so why would I? I can sit in Katamood, kill some rats and fire sprites and the occasional, actually–dangerous thing if I have to. The rest of the time I can complain that there is nothing for a Hero to do."

"You don't really want that."

"It's the best of both worlds. And the public love it."

"But... The good old days."

Rawk grabbed his plate of fish from the serving woman and thumped it down on the table. He hurt his arm. "There are no good old days, Weaver. There are just the days that have gone before." He pulled out his knife and fork and ate his fish in silence. It was disgusting.

Five minutes later, Weaver still sulked, poking at his food and sighing loudly for anyone who wanted to listen.

Rawk sighed too.

"Do you ever regret it?"

"What?"

"The whole 'Prince' thing."

"Of course. My days on the road with you were the best of my life. I never wanted to give that up."

"Then why did you?"

Weaver threw down his fork. "By the time we were twenty years old you were already on your way to being a great. I was good, better than just about anyone left these days, but if I stayed with you I was always going to be your side–kick. I was going to be incidental to the story, no matter what the truth was." He shrugged. "And even if I struck out on my own, I was always going to be compared to you."

"So you became a prince?"

"I wanted to be your equal, and I could never do that as a Hero." He spread his hands. "As a prince though..."

"Lucky there was a city that needed saving then."

"Exactly. If I hadn't come along Katamood would be nothing more than a squalid pirate haven by now."

"Now it's a lovely pirate haven."

"Are you calling me a pirate?"

"You certainly take a lot of money from the owners of ships. And I imagine you'll be trying to take even more soon."

Weaver smiled and gave a small bow from his seat.

"You are a better pirate than I could ever be," Rawk said. "And speaking of money, did you ever pay me back?"

"For what?"

"I loaned you the money for those mercenaries."

"Of course I paid you back."

"You'd better hope so. The interest would just about send you broke."

Weaver smiled some more. "Not even close. In fact, you may want to go find something to kill so you can start to catch up."

"Says the man who rigged the game in his favor."

"I do what I can."

−O−

Rawk wandered along the river with no thought as to where he was or where he was going. After the stench of the *Mermaid's Tail* the stench of the waterfront came as a welcome relief. He wasn't feeling well—he blamed lunch—so at least there was a breeze, even if it smelled of mud and mold.

Across to the south of the river, ships were packed in shoulder-to-shoulder and men, women and dwarves were working frantically to transfer cargo. Everything on the docks seemed to happen at a breakneck pace. Rawk could remember when that had excited him, the sounds and sights and smells of a dozen lands. Now it just left him exhausted. Or perhaps that was lunch as well.

This side of the river also had ships, but not as many and their cargoes were the sort that nobles would not find offensive. Silk from the south. Iron from the north. Haketain from even further north. Much of it would be transferred to wagons and portaged across to Westport so it could be loaded onto more ships and taken further still. But Weaver would collect his taxes and all would be right with the world. Except now there was the canal and dwarves and...

Well, there were going to be dwarves one way or the other. They were the ones who did a lot of the work on the wharves. And Rawk supposed he didn't mind. As long as he didn't have to do it. A life lugging cargo from ships to wagons and wagons to warehouses was the very thing he had run away from when he was fifteen years old. He wondered where he would be if he'd stayed, working beside his father. His knee and back and arm would still be aching, just for different reasons. He wouldn't have half as many interesting stories to tell, but perhaps he would have somebody he wanted to tell them to.

Most importantly, he'd probably know where his father was.

Rawk sat on a wooden post that had once been used to tie up ships and was now nothing more than a salt encrusted, iron—banded decoration. He closed his eyes and breathed.

When he was younger he'd returned home every couple of months. His mother had died when he was barely walking and his father had simply disappeared between one visit and the next. One neighbor said he had died. Another said he had moved away south with a woman from Falangoon. Rawk had looked for him, but the world was a big place. Yardi had always been there.

He sat for a while longer, wondering if he should have made a bigger effort to find out what had happened. His father had been a rough, awkward man, but he had done his best, and Rawk supposed that he hadn't turned out too bad.

"Rawk!"

Rawk opened his eyes and looked around. A man dashed down the street towards him, waving his arms as he dodged through the crowd.

"Rawk."

Rawk sighed. "Yes? What is it?" Someone he didn't know talking to him as if they were old friends.

"You must come." The man stopped close by, heaving in air. He held up a hand as if stopping Rawk from filling the void in the conversation. "There's a..." He put his hands on his knees as he tried to breathe. "There's a demon."

"A demon?"

The stranger nodded.

"Then surely you need a priest, not a Hero."

The man ignored the statement. "It isn't far."

"Then why can't you breathe?"

"I've been looking everywhere for you."

"Did you try the barracks?"

"But you don't go there."

"Soldiers do."

The man gave him a strange look.

Rawk looked around. People were watching. People were always watching. But a demon? He swallowed. "Oh, all right then. Hurry up."

As he followed the man, Rawk tried to think. He had *Kult* with him but there were probably a dozen other things that would have been handy. Like a priest, if it really was a demon.

Further to the east and three blocks back from the river, at the end of a little dead end street, there was a wide, squat house that was shouldering aside the taller buildings around it like a dwarf among elves. A crowd had gathered at a safe distance and were talking quietly as they listened to the wild, gut twisting screech of... something. As Rawk approached a tall gangly man broke away from the others and rushed over.

"Thank Path you're here, Rawk."

"It's your house?"

The man nodded and sucked on the place his front teeth should have been.

"And you saw this demon?"

He nodded. "I think so. Maybe. It's in the roof. I heard a noise up there and stuck my head up through the access panel."

"And you saw it?"

He nodded. "Yes. It darted away into the shadows and started with the wailing."

"Right. And you thought it would be a good idea to get me?"

He shook his head. "I wanted to send for a priest but young Lasten said you were the man to talk to."

"Of course he did."

"Are you going in?"

Rawk looked up at the building. The whole place was in shadow. One of the dormer windows was open a crack. "Why have you got windows in the roof if there are no stairs to get up there?"

The man shrugged. "I didn't build the house. Maybe they were going to extend."

"Right." Everyone was watching him. Of course they were. Could they see how fast his heart was beating? Could they see the sweat? He wiped his hand on his trousers. "Path. Where's the access panel?"

"In the hallway."

Rawk drew *Kult* and entered the house. The first room was the kitchen. There were dirty dishes everywhere and a pile of clothes in the corner. It smelled like something had died there. *Probably food poisoning*, Rawk thought. He wiped his hand again.

There was a chair in the hallway and the open hatchway above. So he climbed on the chair then stepped up again to balance precariously on the back. Once his sword was up in the ceiling space he paused to listen.

The demon still wailed. The sound wasn't any more pleasant from inside. In fact, it was worse. Rawk swore again and pulled himself up to wiggle and squirm into the roof cavity. His arm hurt, but he was too busy looking around to take much notice, If something was going to attack, now would be the worst possible time for that to happen. He got his feet under him and crouched in the dusty space. There was enough space to stand under the peak of the roof but a step to either side and he would hit his head.

"Wonderful. Barely room to swing a sword." Not that he was sure a sword would be any use. "What in Path's name am I doing here?" Once more he'd let the crowd talk him into doing something he didn't want to do. It was too late now. He stepped carefully from ceiling joist to ceiling joist. The wailing increased as he approached. The sound echoed around the ceiling space, but a pile of junk at the far end that was the only possible hiding place...

Rawk paused and took a deep breath. It didn't calm him down at all. He wanted to wipe the sweat from his hand again but didn't dare.

"I hate demons." But when he thought about that, it was just silly. He didn't believe in *demons*. Not in the religious creatures from hell, anyway. He didn't believe in Path, and he didn't believe in hell. So if this was a *demon* it was just another exot. Like the hundreds of others he'd killed in his life. Just an exot.

He started moving again, quicker this time, before he came up with a counter argument.

And two yards from the junk, he paused again. The noise paused too, but only for a moment. When it started again it sounded worse than before. Rawk shifted his grip on *Kult*. He licked his lips. He cleared his throat. He shifted his grip.

"Damn it."

Whatever it was making the noise was only small. A foot high at most. How dangerous could it be? As dangerous as a gabalo, perhaps. Or a cornered weasel. He stepped forward one more joist and reached out with the tip of his sword. He pushed at a timber box. It clattered down from the top of the pile. The wailing paused. For a moment. Then it started again. Rawk picked up a dirty, rotten cloth on the tip of *Kult* and flung it away. He slid a hatbox out of the way.

Movement. There was a screech worse than all those that had come before, as if whoever made it was having its soul rung out by two very angry jesips. A plant pot tumbled to the floor of its own accord.

Rawk squinted into the shadows. He leaned closer. He gave a grunt of laughter and, lowering his sword, stepped forward. The cat, barely more than a kitten stopped its bawling and looked at him with fearful eyes. Rawk picked up the full bag that it was trapped beneath and grabbed it by the scruff of the neck before it could escape.

The creature squirmed and wrestled in his grip, trying to escape, trying to scratch him, until he stood his sword against the gable and petted it. A moment later it had calmed and purred in his arms.

It was mangy and dirty, and smelled, but it was doubtful it had ever been near any type of hell, unless it had been across the other side of the river. "Demon," Rawk said, shaking his head. He pulled out some of his dried snack meat and it disappeared in an instant.

A minute later, Rawk was halfway back to the access panel, the kitten quiet and content for the moment, when he had an idea. He made his way over to the open window and set the kitten down nearby. "Stay there."

It looked at him strangely.

"Seriously, wait there."

Putting his sword down again, Rawk took a deep breath... and screamed. He threw himself towards the window, banging the casement open and hanging half onto the roof. He scrabbled at the tiles. He screamed some more as he pretended he was being dragged back inside.

The crowd screamed with him. They stepped back, staring up in horror. Some of them ran, sprinting away down the street. Rawk managed to contain his laughter as he was 'pulled' inside. He stopped screaming a moment later as he collected the kitten and went back to the window. He stuck his head out into the open and thrust the animal out in front of him.

"It was a cat you idiots." He dropped it onto the roof and it clattered away across the tiles, heading for the building next door. It disappeared into a hole in the wall. "A cat was trapped under a pile of junk." Rawk wanted to say more. He wanted to tell them to think. But he'd been telling people things for years and none of them had ever listened. Don't throw money. Don't throw walnuts. Don't ask for my blessing. They never listened. They never stopped to think about things first.

They were like a bunch of children. The whole city. They never grew up.

Rawk sheathed *Kult* and lowered himself back down into the house. He sat on the chair and rubbed at his face as he realized what he'd done. Firstly, he'd sent half the crowd fleeing into the city. By now there would be a dozen rumors spreading through Katamood. It was unlikely any of them would paint him favorably. And secondly, he'd called those who'd stayed behind 'idiots'. Those people may not paint him favorably either.

The owner of the house disturbed his thoughts, and Rawk realized he didn't care what the man thought. Not now. Not today. He still hadn't helped an old lady cross the street, but he'd rescued a kitten. He wasn't sure which was worse. He rose to his feet. "I would appreciate it if you would make a donation, a donation of money, to the Brothers of Granda."

"But—"

"I am not here to solve every one of your tiny little problems." And he left the house. He pushed through the crowd and headed for home.

Tewsday

RAWK EXAMINED THE STAFF. "Is it supposed to be crooked like that?" he asked, taking his last bite of breakfast.

Travis shrugged. "I like it."

"Yes, but..."

"Look, if you want a straight, soulless piece of wood, go find one yourself. There are plenty of Mindormen down in the market who can make stuff like that. This one was taken from Richnar forest by a dwarf."

"A dwarf?"

"Yes, a dwarf. Does it feel good in your hand?"

Rawk hefted it. It *did* feel good. It looked like a natural piece of wood, polished and varnished, but with knobs and whorls and kinks all left how they were. Despite that, there were several places where his hand fitted perfectly, as if the timber molded to fit. And the weight, no matter where he held it, was comfortable, perfect in one way or another. He gave a reluctant nod.

"Right," Travis said. "I don't like dwarves either. They're loud and obnoxious, but when they want, they know how to do things properly."

"Maybe." But he had been thinking the exact same thing a couple of days earlier.

"Look, just forget that I mentioned dwarves. My grandmother made it, all right."

"I thought your grandmother was dead."

"I didn't say she made it yesterday."

Rawk ran his finger along the grain of the dark timber. "All right, I'll keep it. Just because I don't want to insult the memory of your grandmother. And, also, I don't have time to go and get another one."

"There's an old broom downstairs somewhere. I can break the head of that if you like and you can use the handle."

"Maybe you should go and do some work instead."

Travis started to leave, but turned in the doorway. "So, why are you doing this again?"

Rawk sighed. "Because it's what I do. I don't know anything else."

"Are you sure you still know *this*?" He stayed where he was for a moment, then was gone.

Rawk laid the staff on the bed so he could sling his bag over his shoulder. He checked all the pouches on his belt were secure, slipped *Kult* into the half scabbard, then took up the staff again and followed after Travis.

"Ho, Rawk," Natan said, coming up the other way. "Off on an adventure?"

Rawk put on his Hero face and gave a bark of laughter. "Life is an adventure, Natan. The city may be at risk, and someone has to protect it." He'd never realized that he had a *Hero face*.

"That troll? Do you think there are more of them?"

"I don't know. But I intend to find out."

"Well, good luck. All the luck in the world, for I don't want any trolls disturbing my breakfast."

Rawk hurried the rest of the way down the stairs and headed towards the back door. Out in the ostler's yard, a plain, well–used coach was standing in wait. Horses stamped while men unloaded chests and luggage. Someone staying for a while. Rawk smiled as he slipped out onto the street.

He retraced his steps to Sparrow Tower, trying to ignore the crowd that gathered behind him. Sometimes people called out, asking what he was doing, but most of the time they talked among themselves, speculating as if he wasn't even there. Someone asked him how he had escaped the demon. He didn't reply.

In the mouth of the same alley he'd used the other day, Rawk paused and looked back.

"Thanks you for accompanying me this far," he said, "but this alley isn't big enough for all of us."

The crowd laughed. They'd laugh if he told them about his laundry if they thought it was supposed to be a joke.

"I doubt there will be any spectacle today. I am venturing into the Old Forest to see if there are any more of the trolls. I don't expect to find any, but I want to check, just in case. You are safe, so please, go about your business."

The crowd cheered and half of them followed when he continued on. He suspected the other half were heading for the remains of the wall around Sparrow Tower. The rumors would be spreading through Katamood before the breakfast crowd started to build in the *Hero's Rest*. Rawk was off to save the city again. And the demon hadn't killed him after all.

He paused under the trees a few minutes later, standing in the spot where he had first encountered the troll. The heaviness was upon him again. The ancient watching, like an old owl up in the rafters of a barn.

"What in Path's name *am* I doing here," he muttered to the owl, wherever it was. The 'good old days' were back and he was about to walk blindly into the forest to prove it. What would he have done thirty years ago? First of all, he wouldn't have paused to think.

With a sigh he examined the ground where the fight had started. Squinting, he got down low so his eyes didn't hurt. Everything was a mess there so he widened his search, concentrating to the west and north. But he wasn't a tracker. He wasn't a woodsman. Most of the creatures he killed in the past had come to him. That was the point. If they wanted to be left alone then they never came to his attention in the first place. He searched for half an hour and didn't find any evidence that a huge troll had ever passed by, but he did see what looked like the faint remains of a game trail. That seemed as good a place to start as anywhere else. So he struck deeper into the forest, swatting at the encroaching undergrowth with his staff. Thirty yards in he found a green ribbon caught on a briar thorn.

"Damn." Rawk realized he'd been hoping that he wouldn't find anything. Then he could have turned around and headed home, safe in the knowledge that Hawk Squad wouldn't steal his thunder. Taking the ribbon from the thorn, he tucked it into his pocket and continued forward.

Every step he took, the forest seemed to close in around him. Each tree was thicker than the one before. They were probably taller as well but it was hard to tell through the thick canopy. The light was tinged green but still plentiful. The calls of the animals were muted, but they were plentiful as well.

A minute later, the trail led into the remains of a building. The walls were knee height, the chimney higher. It was a large place, with several rooms and a hollow, depressed area that might once have been a cellar.

Then out through a doorway on the other side and he found himself in the true remains of the city. Buildings, some complete but for the roof, others barely more than a shin high bump, lined either side of dense streets of greenery. There was a well, filled with purple flowers, at an intersection. The blooms overflowed onto the roadway and halfway to one of the buildings. The trail wandered past the other side, skirting over the roots of two huge oak trees, and Rawk didn't see that he had any choice but to follow.

First, he sat with his back against the well, *Kult* laid across his lap, and pulled his bag from beneath his cloak. Inside was a water skin, fruit and a heel of bread. The bread had started to dry out anyway, so he chewed on that first while he sat and rested. After a drink, he thought of eating something else, but he was stalling and knew he should get on with the task at hand.

When he was walking again, following the trail, his sword was back by his side and his staff gripped tightly in his hand. He swatted branches aside with the staff and moved carefully. The trail followed the same street for more than a mile, then turned to the right. Then left at the street after that and deeper into the forest.

Weaver had once shown Rawk a thing called a line graph. It had charted the flow of ships into Katamood over the seasons. The buildings on either side of the street showed the rise and fall of civilizations. It showed man's battle with nature. Nature was winning.

When he had walked for another half an hour, Rawk started to relax. He'd seen a fox, several deer and a handful of rabbits, as well as the usual assortment of birds, but nothing that looked even remotely like a ten-foot tall troll. The city still surrounded him. The walls were still beside him, tall or short, whole or barely there at all, but the streets were wider, the trees were larger and the animals more numerous.

And the arrows were larger. Rawk examined the long white shaft that was stuck in the tree beside him. It was as long as his arm. The fletching was as red as blood. The arrow was still quivering.

"Path." Rawk threw himself to the side as another arrow whistled past. It entered the undergrowth, tearing into the bushes, clattering against a rock.

For a moment, Rawk stayed where he was. He was hidden, but that wouldn't help much if his attacker came looking for him. He grabbed his staff, rearranged his sword and crawled towards remains of the nearest building. At the wall he stopped and stuck his head up above the sea of undergrowth to see what he could see. Trees. He grunted in disgust, though he didn't know what he'd been expecting. Glad to still have his head, he started looking for the doorway so he wouldn't have to go over the top of the wall, even though it was only a foot high. And, once he had some protection, he risked another look.

Trees again. Tall, ancient trees. And... He cocked his head to the side as if that might help.

Rawk gave a small smile. About twenty yards away, a troll was crouching behind an oak tree. It was bigger than the last one, from what he could tell. It had long shaggy hair but none of the ribbons or fetishes. So the other one *was* a shaman then. And this one a warrior.

"Just what I need," Rawk muttered. If the shaman had come close to killing him with nothing more than a tree branch, what would an armed warrior do? It carried a bow that was taller than Rawk and examined the forest with cold, expressionless eyes. It had another arrow ready to go.

Rawk examined his surroundings. Nothing had changed. Forest and ragged walls. He ducked down and wondered what to do next. *I could charge the creature,* Rawk thought, but he wasn't completely serious. Well, seeing he didn't have a bow, he'd have to get closer. So he started to crawl again, pushing through a thick carpet of red flowers. After a few yards he stopped. He didn't think it was a good idea to poke his head up again, so he held his breath instead and tried to listen for sounds of movement. The pounding of his heart made that all but impossible. He crawled some more. When he looked up next, the troll was crouching on the wall, watching. Its bow and quiver were leaning against the wall close by. It held a mace with a solid oak ball the size of Rawk's head. The spikes were as long as his fingers.

"Hello," Rawk said.

The troll sneered. "The forest is not safe, little man."

Rawk got to his knees, leaving his staff on the ground and reaching for the hilt of his sword. *Why the hell did I bring* Kult? he wondered. *I need more reach.* He glanced at the bow. He wondered if he could draw the troll away then race back and collect it. But he'd need to get an arrow as well and then nock it. He'd need a big head start and he doubted he could draw the bow anyway. And he'd never liked bows and therefore had never been very good at using them. Or perhaps it was the other way around. He slowly drew his sword instead. It would look like a dagger in the hand of his opponent. The creature smiled, rose to its feet, and stepped down into the house.

"Path." Rawk backed away, working at the clasp on his cloak. He let the garment fall to the ground then almost tripped over it. The troll closed the distance between them. Rawk shrugged his shoulders to get the bag off. And the troll attacked when the strap got stuck in the folds of his shirt.

Rawk rolled to the side, coming up without the bag. He spun back and lunged. But the troll was somewhere else, faster than should have been allowed for something that large. A moment later, the troll come back at him from behind, swinging high. Duck and slash. The troll lashed out with a boot. Rawk grunted and fell back, stomach aching and probably already bruising, possibly bleeding. He struggled to draw breath as he scrambled backwards. At the wall, he stopped. He didn't have the strength to get himself over the top.

"Great Path." It was an opportune time to start believing in a god. Rawk could feel panic clawing at his chest, squeezing his heart.

His opponent stalked closer, green eyes fierce. It showed big yellow teeth in a snarl of hate.

Rawk got himself partially upright and lurched away. Nobody would see if he ran, nobody would know. His mind rebelled against the thought anyway. They might not see, but he would know. And, as with the wolf, he knew that running was useless. He wouldn't get far. He wouldn't have gotten far even before being kicked.

In the corner he turned to fight. The troll was on him almost before he was ready. He slid the first swing of the mace past his shoulder. Barely. He stepped around the next and darted forward. But the troll's strength was amazing. It stopped the huge weapon with seemingly no effort and reversed the swing. Rawk managed to keep his head as he stumbled away.

Flowers tripped him up. A sharp rock jarred his knee when he fell. He almost called out. Noises behind him made him turn his fall into a not–very–effective roll and he landed on his back. He batted away another attack and knew it was a mistake before he'd even finished. He started to roll again as *Kult* shattered. The troll's mace thudded into the ground beside his head. He spat dirt. Flowers rained down around him a second later. He scrambled away, fingers in the dirt, trying to pull himself forward quicker. *Quicker. Quicker.* Never quick enough.

All he could hear was the thundering of his heart. He could smell flowers. He didn't know what they were called but they looked a bit like pennylace.

He tried to concentrate, to keep his mind on more important matters, to think. He kept moving, up to his elbows and knees in the unknown flowers.

The troll must have been getting sick of the game for it followed close behind.

Rawk crawled and limped and scrambled, looking over his shoulder, breathing in the stench of the flowers.

He stumbled, slipped, was drawing in the smell, face in the dirt. As he tried to get back up, his hands touched something. His fingers closed and he recognized the perfect, comfortable feel of his new dwarven staff. He tripped again, rolled. On his back, he saw the troll over him, mace swinging before it was even within range.

Rawk brought the staff up out of the pool of flowers, spun the pointed end around. The troll was caught by surprise. It tried to stop its charge, but Rawk lunged forward and the staff sank into the creature's eye.

But the mace kept coming, momentum swinging it around. Rawk winced and waited for the blow, unable to do anything about it. Soil flew again and that contact with the ground was all that saved him. The blow deflected, slowed. A spike tore through the flesh on his arm. The troll landed on top of him and almost crushed his leg. It might have broken it anyway.

Rawk screamed out in pain. He only did it once though, so he was quite pleased with himself, in his moments of lucidness.

He woke some time later. He didn't know how long.

"I'm starting to make a habit of this." He gritted his teeth against the pain. He was a lot further from help this time.

Rawk looked at his arm first. The mace's spike was still there, impaling the flesh, but not as bad as he'd imagined. He didn't want to remove it because that would increase the bleeding but he really didn't have any choice. Taking a deep breath, he grabbed the handle of the mace and carefully, slowly, pushed it away from him so the spike slid out of his arm. It hurt. He gritted his teeth against the pain, closing his eyes for a moment while he got control of his breathing. He sat up with a groan of pain and saw blood streaming down his arm. At least it seemed to be. A healer might have had a different word for it. Trickling? Dribbling? And his feet were shouting complaints. He chose to ignore them, as best he could. One problem at a time.

Rawk tore strips off his shirt. He wadded up the first to block the wound. The second he used as a bandage, awkwardly wrapping it around his arm and tying it off. It wasn't very tight, but it would have to do.

He tried to calm his thundering heart.

Next task. The troll was still on his legs. It wasn't going to be easy to move. Rawk gave the problem some thought. Anything to keep his mind off the pain. Anything to stop him wondering how long he had left to live. Anything to stop him from looking around to see if the troll had any friends.

The dwarf staff had come free and was laying close by, still in one piece. Rawk took it up and slid it underneath the troll's corpse.

I'm about to find out how strong this really is, he thought. Once it was all the way through, he got the tip onto the ground and started to lever the troll away from his legs. The creature shifted a little bit. Then a bit more.

Finally, Rawk raised the staff just enough to slide the troll down to the ground. He worked his way out from under an arm and breathed a sigh of relief. His arm hurt, his leg hurt and his stomach and ribs still ached. At least it was his left arm again. And he didn't think any of them were life threatening, now that he had a moment to think.

He looked around to see if the troll had any friends.

There *was* someone there, though Rawk couldn't see who.

Rawk took a guess and waved. "Hello, Deaner," he said. He would look silly if he was wrong, but that couldn't be helped.

The Captain of Hawk Squad came out from behind a tree five yards from the one he was looking at. Close enough.

"Rawk? Is that you?"

"Who else would it be?"

"Well..."

"I could do with a hand here, you know."

"What happened?" The Captain came closer. "We could hear noises but couldn't work out what the hell..." He stepped up onto the low wall and came to a stop, staring at the troll. "You killed another one?"

"I would've let you do it if you'd arrived a bit sooner." Rawk took a deep breath. "Could I borrow your healer for a few minutes?"

—O—

Rawk almost fell out of the wagon as he tried to climb out over the side.

Deaner hadn't been happy to just leave him standing by the side of the road, just a few yards from the wall. But Rawk had insisted. Hawk Squad could not help but draw attention and if anyone recognized the limping, bruised man with them that would have been the end of it. So he had thanked them and started slowly down the street. That seemed like days ago but could not have been more than and hour. He didn't know how far he'd walked before someone had taken pity on him and offered him a ride. It was a dwarf, but he'd accepted anyway. That seemed like days ago too.

Rawk gathered his thoughts, it wasn't easy, and looked up at the driver. "Thank you," he croaked.

The dwarf grunted, then shook the reins to get the horses moving again. Rawk pulled his hood further down over his face.

"Are you all right?" someone asked.

He nodded and waved them on. "I'm fine. Just a little under the weather." He wasn't dying. Probably. Just very sore all over and just about as tired as he had ever been in his life.

"Are you sure?"

He waved again and leaned against the wall, cradling his arm and favoring his foot. He noticed, through his haze of pain, more *Words of Wisdom*, painted on the side of the building across the other side of the road. *The darkness will always end, but if morning is too far away, light a torch.*

Rawk tried to work out what that meant. Did it mean anything at all? Thinking about it made his head hurt so he pushed himself upright and staggered the final steps of his journey, down the hill towards Sylvia's door. It was fifty yards, with half a dozen stairs, and almost beyond him. He stumbled in through the door, wincing as the bell rang above his head. Sylvia was talking to a customer in the front room so Rawk straightened up as best he could and made his way to the stool by the counter. He sat down heavily and tried to arrange himself so he didn't look like he was about to die. Then he waited and tried not to die.

Breathing helped. The dry crisp air of the room was probably filled with all types of medicine, kicked up as Sylvia mixed the concoctions. He was probably being cured of a dozen things he didn't even know he had.

Finally, the old lady handed over a couple of copper coins, took a small jar from Sylvia, and made her way out onto the street.

Rawk slumped onto the counter as soon as the door closed.

"What has happened?" Sylvia rushed over and stopped him from falling any further. "Come with me." She supported him as she led the way towards the door to the back of the shop.

"Thank you."

"What have you been doing?"

Rawk didn't answer until he had climbed up onto a high timber bed and laid down with a grateful sigh.

"The same as usual," he said. "Saving the city and all that."

"Really? Have you ever actually saved the city before?"

Rawk tried to think as he pushed his cloak away from his arm. "No. I don't think so. There were those rats..."

Sylvia started to laugh, but cut off when she saw the blood on his arm. "This certainly wasn't done by a rat."

"Another troll."

"*Another* troll?" She hurried over to a shelf. She searched for a moment before finding a powder and mixing it with water from a jug on a table.

Rawk tried a smile but it didn't feel right.

"Here, drink this. All of it."

As Sylvia rushed off again, getting bandages and a needle, Rawk drank. It tasted horrible, which was to be expected.

"Are there more? Where are they coming from?" Sylvia started working on his arm. Rawk tried not to watch what she was doing.

"Are you one of Thacker's spies?"

Sylvia attempted a smile then. "I will certainly let him know."

"Well, let him know that they look like trolls, but I don't know for sure."

"Dwarves know a bit about trolls. If Thacker or one of his scholars could—"

"Wait, Thacker's a dwarf?"

"Of course. What did you think?"

"Well, I thought he was human, obviously."

Sylvia shook her head. "There are nearly three times as many dwarves living on the South side of the river as there are humans. And there are more elves than humans as well. Do you think *we* would follow a human?" Sylvia sighed. "This wound it not good, Rawk. Half an inch to the side and I would have been amputating."

"*We?*"

"Pardon?"

"You said 'we'. As in, 'we elves'."

"Everyone thinks elves and dwarves are some type of mortal enemy from centuries ago—which isn't true, we just never understood each other—but *nobody* can understand humans."

"*We* elves? You're an elf?"

Sylvia stopped working at Rawk's arm and looked at him. For a moment she smiled, as if at some grand joke, but then seemed to realize that he really didn't know. She laughed. "All these years and you didn't know?"

"If I'd known..."

"You wouldn't have come to me for help? Or you would have tried harder to kill me previously? Or perhaps you wouldn't have lowered yourself to battle me at all. Are you less of a man because you couldn't defeat an elf?"

Rawk's face reddened. He started to sit up, but Sylvia pushed him back down. He was so weak he couldn't fight her.

"How ever did you survive all these years, Rawk? You walk around in a daze, seeing the world as you want it to be."

"If I saw the world as I wanted it to be there wouldn't be any elves or dwarves at all."

She fetched an ointment down from a shelf and came back to the bed, shaking her head. "You think humans are better than the other races, when really we come from the same people."

Rawk spluttered. "We do not."

"I am not a full elf, Rawk. My mother was an elf. My father was a human, a logger from a little village a few days north of Fadanel."

"You're still an elf."

She sighed. "I'm not trying to get into your good books by claiming to be a human. 'We elves', remember? What I'm saying is that humans and elves, and dwarves, can all interbreed. There are no abnormalities with the offspring. We are the same people."

"We are not."

"We cannot breed with Nokins. We can breed with Galangs but the offspring are always mules. Humans and elves *are* the same breed. The fermi and the Katans divided some time ago, before recorded history, but humans, elves and dwarves divided even before that."

"Dwarves are hardly more than animals. They—"

"Grow up, Rawk. Think for once in your life instead of spitting forth the same tired lines that Heroes have been spitting for thousands of years."

"They stink worse than a pen full of dead pigs."

"They smell, so they are animals?"

"They don't smell. They *stink*."

"Where do you see these dwarves? The stinky ones?"

"All through the city."

"North of the river?"

"Of course. I never come south."

"And what are the dwarves doing? The ones north of the river?"

"Working on the sewers. Cleaning the streets. Building things. They stank up the *Hero's Rest* for more than a month."

"So they're working?"

"Yes."

"These *men* are doing hard physical work, often for twelve hour shifts, and you are complaining that they smell?"

"Well..."

"Have you seen them at home? After work?"

"Of course. Not at home, but when they aren't working."

"When they are walking home from work?"

"Are you done yet?"

She tied off a bandage with a violent tug. "I don't know, am I?"

"The troll kicked me in the stomach and ribs and then landed on me."

"Are you sure you want an elf looking at that?" Sylvia sighed and went back to work. She probed his stomach with long, strong fingers. Rawk tried not to move. "Nothing is broken. There is no serious damage that I can see."

"Oh. All right then. It hurts like hell."

"Live with it. Anything else?"

"Fine." He tried to think of anything else. *Maybe...* "There's something wrong with my knee, too."

Sylvia sighed and knelt on the floor. She poked and prodded around the joint, moving the leg backwards and forwards.

"I think you need to find another healer, Rawk. I refuse to help a man who seems intent on getting himself killed."

Rawk grunted. "I think you don't really understand what choices I do and don't have, Silver Lark."

"What, Weaver is forcing you?"

He shook his head. "I'm a Hero; I have to do Heroic things. That means I can't sit around in a tavern while Hawk Squad run around the forest hunting trolls. I won't get any respect for that."

"Respect from whom, Rawk? Those people who fawn over you? They are the same ones that cheer at a public flogging. Maybe you should give some thought to who you are trying to impress." She paused in her ministrations and looked up. "The troll did this to you?"

Rawk cleared his throat. "When it fell on me."

She didn't say anything, but gave him a look that clearly said what she thought of that. She collected a jar from a shelf and set it down on a bench. "Rub that on every morning."

Rawk didn't say anything. He started to push himself upright.

"Don't be stupid. You'll be staying here for a while so I can keep an eye on you."

"I can't..."

What he couldn't do was sit up. He slumped back down. "How long do I have to stay?"

"We'll see."

Wensday

RAWK STARTED TO ROLL OVER and almost fell off the bed. He looked around at the medicines and drugs and scrolls. There were noises from out the front of the shop as Sylvia served a customer. She came through the door a few minutes later, pushing her long hair away from her face and hooking it behind an ear.

"I wasn't sure if you were going to wake up."

"I didn't know I needed to." He groaned as he pushed himself into a sitting position. He could see that her ear was a little bit pointy, now that he looked.

"Once the medicine took effect it didn't take long."

"I thought you might have used magic."

"We had that conversation before."

"Well, I can hope."

"You can, but it won't help."

"How long *was* I asleep?"

"Almost an entire day."

Rawk felt like he could sleep for another day. He watched as Sylvia did a quick check of the dressing on his arm. There didn't appear to be any blood.

"Do you have any of the tea remaining?"

"Yes."

"Well, here's some more anyway. Pack this new wound tonight as well. You opened the other one up again, by the way. You need to rest the arm."

"I was resting it. I was using the other arm."

"Grow up, Rawk. Now get out of my shop before I need to bring someone out here. And don't forget the cream for your knee."

Rawk got himself upright and shrugged awkwardly into his cloak. Out the front, the doorbell clanged as somebody entered the shop.

"You'd better go out the back," Sylvia said.

"Right." He grabbed his belongings without looking and crossed to the door at the back of the room as quickly as he could.

"And Rawk..."

He stopped with his hand on the door handle. "Yes?"

"Send Travis around with my money later. Fifty ithel, and I'm doing you a favor."

Rawk sneered. "Right."

Out in the alley he tried to get himself organized. He went to sheath *Kult* but noticed that there wasn't much more than a stub of the blade left. He remembered something about that. "Path." He'd had the sword for a long time. Since almost the beginning. He'd taken it from a Merindoc prince killed by a band of brigands outside Jilk. Rawk hadn't been paid to protect him, but he felt guilty about the death and the sword both. In the alley, a long tired lifetime away from Jilt, he rammed the stub into its sheath and swung his pack over his shoulder. His arm ached all over and Rawk didn't know if he'd be able to fight another troll even if he wanted to.

The first thing he had to do, before he went off looking for more trolls, was visit Weaver. Ramaner was going to shout at him as it was. *Why didn't you come to us yesterday?* Rawk sighed and started limping down the hill, trying to avoid crowds so he wouldn't get jostled.

Then again, maybe Weaver could wait.

–O–

Rawk woke with a start. His arm ached from shoulder to wrist. His leg ached. His head ached. With a deep breath he rolled over and got his feet on the floor. They hurt too.

It was a moment before he noticed that Travis was sitting on the floor near the door. He had a jug of steaming water ready to go and started to work before Rawk had levered himself upright.

"Don't you knock?"

"I did."

"Oh."

"I was going to leave if you didn't wake up soon."

"No stamina."

"The water is getting cold."

"What time is it?"

"Lunch time. I think you pretty much walked up stairs and went to sleep."

"I needed it. I feel better now, but... Path, I was tired."

Rawk knelt down with his head over the bowl and Travis laid the towel over his head then set to work on the wound on his upper arm, carefully unwrapping the bandage then packing it with drained tealeaves from the jug.

"You were lucky."

"Lucky? I was nearly killed by a harien troll. How in Path's name is that lucky?"

"A harien troll? Never heard of it."

"That's what the bock calls it."

"That book you were reading the other night?"

"No, another book from my vast collection."

"Well, I wasn't sure if you'd made it past the title."

Rawk sneered but it was wasted under the towel. He changed the subject. "I forgot to ask, how did you go at the club the other night?" He winced when Travis shoved some more tea onto his arm. "That well, hey."

"It was great."

"Look, Travis—"

"No. Just shut up and breathe."

Rawk stopped talking and took a deep breath.

"It was all right," Travis said when he started working on the other bandage. "We... I don't know. I think I ruined everything."

"You make being an adult sound like so much fun. I can't think of why I haven't tried it sooner."

Travis packed the drained leaves onto the latest wound. "You risk your life every time you go out to face a monster, Rawk—"

"Did I ever tell you about the musket bamak?" All he'd risked with that monster was sneezing because of all the ridiculous fur. Nobody knew that though.

"Shut up, Rawk. You risk your life all the time, knowing that the reward at the end is worth the risk."

"So?"

"And yet you can't see that the bigger risks in other parts of your life would bring greater rewards as well."

Travis finished packing the second wound so Rawk pulled the towel away from his head and sat up. "Like what? A woman to nag me about coming home too late and drinking too much? Children tripping me up wherever I walk and asking constant questions?"

Travis shook his head. "The only time you drink alcohol is when you think it would ruin your image to do otherwise. And you already have a whole city that follows you around and asks questions all day."

Rawk thought about that for a second. "Right, so why would I want to add someone else to that?"

"Why? I don't know. You'd have to take a risk to find out."

"And what woman would want me anyway, Travis? Not knowing if I'm going to come back each time I go out. All the women throwing themselves at me."

"Of course. Rawk the great Hero. Conqueror of beast and women alike. Why would he give up either of those things?"

"Nothing good ever comes of love, Travis."

"What? A couple of days ago you were saying that I'm too old to be waiting. And if I stand still too long I'll drop dead."

"That's you, Travis. I'm a completely different story." Rawk cleared his throat.

"You are already growing up, Rawk. For some reason, you just don't want other people to know about it."

"Did you bring something to drink?"

"No."

Rawk looked at the wounds on his arm. If he moved too much the tea would fall away. "Do you want to go and get me something?"

"No. I'll be back in a little while to help bandage those up again."

"You can't just leave me here."

Rawk watched as Travis did just that.

"Well..." Rawk *really* needed a drink. He picked up the jug and looked inside. There was still water in there. He swished it around, examining the tealeaves that Travis hadn't been able to fish out. He sniffed, though he already knew perfectly well what is smelt like after breathing the fumes for the last ten minutes.

"Path." He raised the jug to his mouth and took a small, careful sip. He licked his lips and spat out a tiny piece of leaf. He took another sip. If it was poison, he hoped it was the poison of choice for whoever tried to kill him. It tasted good.

Rawk felt himself relaxing even more. He took a drink and closed his eyes.

After a few minutes he roused himself. He rose carefully, not wanting to upset the tealeaves on his arm, and headed for the bed. He'd only taken one step when he noticed a cane chair in the corner of the room. He grunted and changed direction. Someone must have been reading his mind. Again.

Travis returned a few minutes later. "Ready to rewrap your arm?" He handed over a flask of water.

"I guess." Rawk put the water down on the floor.

"You don't want it now?"

"I've been drinking that."

"The tea?"

"Yeah. It's good. Even better than breathing the fumes."

Travis looked doubtful. He worked on the arm as he gave it some thought. "Are you sure it's safe?"

"Not a clue." Rawk winced as Travis finished tying off the bandage.

"Too tight?"

"No. All good. Surprisingly good, actually."

"Ready for another fight, then?"

Rawk grunted. "If I have to. I could eat a horse before that though."

"We've run out of horse. We're onto the dogs now."

"Well, get me at least four of them, then. I'll be down soon."

−O−

Rawk took out his knife and fork and set them on the table as he looked around the taproom. When his lunch came, he went to work and didn't look up for some time. When he did, he was surprised to see someone standing anxiously by his table. It wasn't a soldier, which made a nice change, or a woman which was... something... and it took Rawk a moment to work out who it was. In the end, the huge book in his hand gave the man away.

"Juskin, isn't it?"

"Yes. Yes, it is."

Rawk sat back and wiped his knife and fork on the cloth. He packed them away before he forgot. "What can I do for you today? You don't strike me as the kind of man who spends his days in taverns."

Juskin looked around as if just realizing where he was. "No. I should be in my shop. I have been looking for you all morning."

The old man didn't seem like the type to chase Heroes around the city either. "Well..."

"I was told you normally have lunch at the *Golden Wheel* on Wensdays."

"I do. But not today."

"So I see." He repositioned his spectacles while he looked around again, then slipped into the seat opposite Rawk without being asked.

"Ahhh..."

"I was in the markets this morning. Stall holders often have no idea about the value of their stock and I can make a huge profit if I resell."

Rawk raised his eyebrows.

Juskin laughed. "Relatively huge, of course."

"Of course."

"Anyway, I was looking this morning, as I said, and came across a book I thought you might be interested in."

"What gives you that idea?"

Juskin looked at the book in his hands, then carefully laid it on the table and spun it around for Rawk to see.

"*Encyclopedia of Myth*?"

"Yes. It is quite a bit better than the *Compendium*."

"Great."

"No, really. I have marked the page."

Rawk sighed. "I've had enough of books. That other one is still giving me a headache."

"Are you sure that isn't from being hit on the head?"

"If you are trying to make me read you aren't—"

"I saw the picture of the troll in the newspaper," Juskin said. "It wasn't a lot like the one in the *Compendium*." He opened up the book. "This one, however..."

Rawk looked at the picture. He blinked, hoping his eyes would adjust quickly. He sat back slightly so he was further from the page. It was a much better drawing than the last one. And there was no doubting it was the same as the creatures he'd killed. But it had a different name. He pushed his plate out of the way, and pulled the book closer. And he waited again, pretending to read.

"Duen Giant?" he said eventually.

"I suppose it is impossible to be certain, but it seems a better likeness than the one in Magan's book. That is, of course, as long as the dwarf who drew the picture for the newspaper is a skilled artist."

"A dwarf?"

"Yes. At least I assume so. The newspaper is produced by dwarves."

"Path. Can't they ever mind their own business?"

"This is everyone's business, Rawk, wouldn't you say? Creatures that have not been seen for hundreds of years are returning to Katamood."

"So, what does it say, then?"

"I haven't read it in detail. I just saw that there was a lot of information. Several pages of it."

Rawk read. "*Duen Giants roamed the lands north of Manapee more than two thousand years ago. Wherever they went, violence followed. It is suggested they were almost constantly involved in conflicts, across the breadth of the continent, including the Battle of Hapahide and the Siege of Makanua Rock that was remembered in the famous folk song of the same name. It seems they were nomadic, presumably in order to find more enemies to battle.*"

There was more, but Rawk closed the book. He ran his hand over the cracked leather of the cover. There was a tree of some kind stamped there, below the title. "So this is better than the other book?"

Juskin shrugged. "I have never heard of the author, but... It *seems* better, wouldn't you say?"

"You're the expert." But it *did* look much better. Though that didn't mean much. There were thousands of swords in the world that looked better than *Kult* but he wouldn't swap for any of them. Well, maybe he would now. "I'll take it off your hands, one way or the other. How much?"

Juskin gave it some thought. "A hundred ithel."

Rawk narrowed his eyes. "We just agreed that it is better than the last one."

Juskin nodded. "Better for your purposes doesn't mean it is worth more in a monetary sense."

"It normally does when you're haggling."

Juskin smiled. "Usually when buyers haggle they try to get the lowest price possible, Rawk."

"Yes, and sellers try to get the *highest* price. So, now I want to know what your angle is."

The old man shrugged. "I want you to come to me next time you need a book. And the time after that. And besides, I only paid forty ithel for it."

"Huge profits?"

"Not terrible for one morning's work, wouldn't you say?"

"Well, I don't have 100 ithel on me right now."

Juskin waved the comment away. "I trust you. And I know where you live."

"I could be killed by a troll tomorrow."

"Or a duen giant."

"Or one of them."

"That's a risk I'm willing to take. I'll start an account for you."

"Thank you. Would you like a drink?"

"No, thank you. My shop has been closed for long enough already." And with that, he rose to his feet and wound his way across to the door.

Rawk opened the book to the duen giants again.

There were pictures on the initial page, a male and a female. The both held weapons, but their expressions were blank, as if the artist was unwilling to commit, unwilling to give the creatures a life of their own when he only had stories to work from.

Rawk turned the page. There were two more pictures. One was... He sat up. One was of a child. A girl, with ribbons and fetishes in her long, shaggy hair. Apart from the blank expression she could have been the one that Rawk had killed by the edge of the forest.

"Path." He swallowed. "A child?" He pushed the book away. *I killed a child?* He'd done similar things in the past, but this time it felt different. He didn't know why.

The damn dog was probably a pet...

Rawk jumped when a newspaper slapped down on the table in front of him.

"For Path's sake, Weaver, don't do that."

"Don't do that? Really? I'll stop when you stop."

"Stop what?"

"You killed another troll."

"Oh, right. I was going to see you, but I'm not feeling all that great at the moment."

Weaver looked around the taproom and quickly sat down. "You probably deserved to die, Rawk," he whispered fiercely. "And then what?"

Rawk looked around too. Ramaner was at a table near the door with two other Guards. "What does it matter to you?"

"What does it matter to me? Really? What does it matter to me?" He took a deep breath and tried to calm himself. "I'm trying to run a city here, Rawk. I'm trying to..."

"Yes? You're trying to run a city and I'm trying to make a living as a Hero."

"Make a living?"

"The troll is dead. That's all that matters isn't it?"

"It is *not* all that matters." He unfolded the newspaper and slapped it down again. It wasn't nearly as dramatic the second time.

"How often do they make these things?"

"I don't know."

"Are you the only person who gets them?"

"What? No, of course not. There are thousands."

Rawk looked at the paper and all the neat lines of writing. "But how do they do all that writing? I only killed the troll yesterday."

"I don't know. And I don't care. Just read the damn thing."

Rawk blinked rapidly, trying to get his eyes to adjust. *"Once again, Rawk has come to Katamood's* rescue, venturing far into the Old Forest, seeking more of the trolls that would threaten the fair city. Prince Weaver had the same thought, sending Hawk Squad to do some searching of their own, but Rawk did not trust them to do the job right. He went out on his own, knowing that stealth would be needed if he was to find any more of the trolls. And a few miles beyond the edges of the forest, he came across one of the foul creatures.

"By the time Hawk Squad arrived, the battle was all but done. Rawk was gravely injured but fought valiantly while Hawk Squad lurked at a safe distance, waiting for the final moment. When it was done, Prince Weaver's men rushed in to help our Hero back to the city and the careful ministrations of a healer."

"That isn't how it happened," Rawk said.

"The newspaper says it was."

Rawk grunted. "And you believe it?"

"I don't see why I wouldn't."

"Yes, well..."

"So now, apparently, you are better than Hawk Squad. The *entire* Hawk Squad combined, mind you. Perhaps that's why they hung back, waiting for you to be killed."

"They didn't hang back."

"They were obviously trying to get rid of the competition."

"I didn't write the damn story." Rawk looked at the newspaper again and at some of the other things written in it. The work on the canal was ahead of schedule but the sewers were behind. A ship from Hadron had docked yesterday bringing news of war in the north. Though that wasn't news as there was always war in the north. Plans for the Summer Fete were going well. And the Veteran's Club had asked Celeste and Grint to come and perform for a few more nights.

It didn't say where the newspaper came from or who had written any of the stories.

"I never said you *wrote* it," Weaver said.

Rawk looked at him and saw the look on his face. "Hey, I never talked to anyone about it either. I came straight here from Janas' place and didn't stop to chat along the way. I've hardly been down stairs since."

"Janas is dead, Rawk."

"I know she is, Weaver. I don't see your point."

Weaver sat down as well. "So, now what *am* I supposed to do?"

Rawk folded up the newspaper. "Have a drink?"

"Are there more? And where are they?"

Rawk sighed. "I still say we aren't about to be overrun by these things. There might be another couple, but it won't be anything your men can't handle."

Weaver didn't look sure.

"This one was bigger than the first one, Weaver, and meaner, but I still managed to kill it on my own."

"You nearly died."

"It fell on me."

"Deaner says you stabbed it with a staff."

"It had a longer reach than my sword. You're full of not having a point today, aren't you? Anyway, all that stuff supports my argument that the first one was a shaman, actually."

"One was big and mean so it's a warrior and the other was small so it was a shaman?"

"Something like that."

"Old Mother Farel's so small she must be a shaman, then. I'll let her know she can call on the spirits to help her cook dinner in future."

"It might help. You never know."

There was a long pause before Weaver spoke again. "And how did you best the warrior, Rawk?" He leaned closer and put his hand on Rawk's knee. "A suicidal charge that wasn't suicidal after all?"

Again, Rawk thought of telling the truth. *I was crawling along the ground, chin deep in flowers, when I came across a weapon I'd dropped earlier in my panic. I spun about as the troll was attacking and caught it by surprise. I got lucky.* And he wondered how detailed Deaner's report had been "You remember that mistamil in Hagamon?" he said instead.

Weaver thought for a moment. "Of course. You threw your sword up into the air and when the beast watched, it was blinded by the sun for a moment."

"Right. Same thing. Except this time I ran in and stabbed it with my staff."

"You used a second sword on the mistamil."

"I didn't *have* a second sword this time. Just my staff."

"Of course, of course. Just like old times, hey, Rawk."

"Then it fell on me," Rawk said. That bit was true.

Weaver nodded but wasn't paying attention. "Maybe I should get a secret passage. I want to fight those creatures that threaten our good people. I want to get out there with you."

"Well, get digging."

"I have people to do that kind of thing for me."

"Not much of a secret then, is it?" Rawk sighed. "Anyway, you're too late."

"Too late for what? There could be other things out there. Dragons or... I don't know. Anything."

"Yes, but I've retired."

"What? When?"

"Just before you arrived. I'm done."

"But... You can't."

"Yes, I can. I just did."

"No, seriously, you can't. This is what we were talking about, the good old days coming back again. When being a Hero meant something. When there were real Heroic deeds to be done. You can't just quit when it's all coming good." Weaver leaned forward in his chair. "I need you to go and see if there are any more trolls."

Rawk wasn't sure he'd heard properly. His eyes narrowed. "Not long ago you were complaining about the last one that I killed. Send Hawk Squad out there."

"The people are already starting to worry. They are talking as if there's a whole... flock... army..."

"I think trolls come in packs, but these ones might not be trolls anyway."

"Either way, there was almost a riot south of the river yesterday. I had to send in the Guard. If I send Hawk Squad out into the forest again that will just stir everything up more."

"So, you want me to sneak out and see what I can see?"

"You don't have to sneak. You're Rawk, you do all sorts of crazy things."

Rawk shook his head. "No, thank you."

"I'll double the bounty."

"Double nothing is still nothing."

"Triple. And I'll pay a thousand ithel even if you don't find anything."

"Look—"

"Just this one more time. If there's nothing there, you can retire."

"I can retire now. I could have retired just before you turned up if I'd wanted... Oh, wait, I did."

"The city needs you, Rawk."

"It does not."

"One last time. You know I'll keep annoying you until I get what I want."

Rawk sighed. He knew Weaver was telling the truth. He wouldn't get a moment of peace. "Oh, all right. I'll go and have a look tomorrow."

"Good. Excellent."

"Triple the bounty."

"I didn't—"

"You bloody well did."

Weaver held up a hand. "All right. Triple."

Before the Prince had even left the room, Rawk decided he really would be crazy to go out into the forest on his own when there could be a whole family of duen waiting for him. He'd share the glory, and the money. That was a very grown up thing to do. Travis and Sylvia would be proud. He'd have a quick look at the newspaper then see what he could organize.

The story about Celeste and her damn dwarf brother was on the back page. There was a sketch of the two of them and everything. "*Mount Grace's own Celeste and Grint are making a name for themselves on the north side of the river. The manager of the Veteran's Club, a venue that rivals even Harker's Hall, has asked them back for another week. Rumor has it that they may be moved into the main theatre and tickets sold to non-members for the first time in living memory.*

"*It is interesting to see non-humans being acknowledged like this but only time will tell if this recognition extends to other areas.*"

–O–

Rawk was taking a shortcut through an alley when he heard a noise behind him. He knew who it was before he even turned around. "Hello, Edwin. I've been expecting you."

Adalee's father was a short man with a bald patch on the top of his head and too much weight around the middle. If he'd ever been in an alley before it was only because he'd been lost.

He nodded. "We need to have a word."

Rawk looked pointedly at the two men standing at Edwin's back. They looked like they knew quite a bit about alleys. One was a huge, with wild hair and a crooked nose. The other was tall and slim and had a scar on his cheek. At least they were carrying cudgels, not knives and swords. Rawk heard a noise in the other direction. He didn't bother turning to count. Two or three at most. Rawk had *Dabaneera*; he thought he could take them, one way or the other. "A word?"

Edwin nodded. "You can think of Havin and his friends as punctuation marks, if you like."

Rawk couldn't help but smile. "That's nice. I like it."

A smile fluttered at the corner of Edwin's mouth as well.

"Before you speak though, may I say something?"

Edwin shook his head and motioned to his followers. "Don't kill him, Havin. Just embarrass him. A lot."

Rawk drew his sword. "I don't want to kill anyone," he said. He'd heard about Havin. The man was supposed to be good at his job.

Scar Face rushed forward but he was only a decoy. Rawk ignored him. He ducked and spun, hitting the man behind him with the flat of his sword. Then back to the decoy. The other man was standing still, looking surprised, and Rawk took the opportunity to slash him across the thigh, just enough for some pain and blood. In the noisy, cursing moments that followed, Rawk got his back against the wall. He cleared a circle on the rough, dark cobbles, kicking away trash so he wouldn't trip. Something had died there recently. His efforts set free a terrible stench that seemed to fill the narrow space in an instant.

"Do you think I lived this long by being bad at what I do?" he asked Havin, trying to gain some extra time. He shifted his grip on his sword; his hand was slick with sweat.

The big man grunted but gave a grudging nod of respect. Rawk wouldn't be able to surprise them again. Three to go. Four if you counted Edwin, but that remained to be seen.

Two more came at him slowly, one from each side.

"I know Yardi Kepeta," Rawk said to Edwin, watching the men, trying to learn as much as he could in the few moments he had.

"So?" Edwin looked suspicious.

"I was talking to her about the Melaworth contracts." Rawk darted forward and slapped at a hand. The thug yelped and dropped his cudgel. He probably wouldn't be holding anything at all for a while.

Havin was about to join the fight, looking none to pleased at the prospect, but Edwin held up a jewel–encrusted hand. His cheek twitched. "And what?"

"I could have a word with her. We've been friends for about fifty years." Rawk tried to slow his breathing.

"But she has not gotten to where she is by doing favors."

"I'm not guaranteeing she'll listen but... She said your tender was really close."

Edwin signaled again and the two thugs stood down "How close?"

Rawk shrugged and Edwin gave the matter some thought.

"I could... Will she listen if I take an ithel per ton off the storage price?"

"The way she was talking, that would probably be enough to get you across the line."

"But the tenders have closed."

"Fifty years."

"And if it isn't enough?"

"Well, you can take it on trust that I tried, or you can go look up Havin again. And find some extra men."

Edwin rubbed at his bald pate. "Path." He didn't look happy. "Thank you for your time, Havin. Take your men and go."

"We're getting paid?"

"Of course."

Havin and his companion helped the casualties from the alley and Rawk wondered if he should send them in Sylvia's direction.

"You were winning, Rawk," Edwin said when they were alone.

"I know. I usually do." He didn't think he would have beaten Havin, not without killing him.

"Then why?"

"I wasn't trying to offend anyone or make enemies. I can understand that you would be upset, so I wanted to try to work something out without resorting to violence." *Which is about the first time that has ever happened.* "If I had known who Adalee was, I can assure you I wouldn't have—"

"You would have found someone else's daughter?"

Rawk thought Edwin was being a little unfair. He never forced the women to go to bed with him. He usually didn't have to work all that hard at all. "Probably, yes. And probably nobody would have been offended." He wasn't about to say that the girl had come looking for *him*. It wasn't the type of thing a father wanted to hear.

"So, I get the contract and you stay away from my daughter?"

"Of course."

Edwin looked around, rubbed his head again. "How do I know you're telling the truth?"

"You'll find out soon enough if I'm lying."

"Do you know how much that contract it worth?"

"Not a clue."

He gave a small, thoughtful nod. "I don't like you, Rawk."

"You don't have to. And just in case, I'll make sure the contract makes mention of my health."

"I'm a man of my word."

"I believe you. So am I."

Edwin's face was hard and cold. "This doesn't get back my daughter's honor."

"No, it doesn't."

He walked out of the alley without looking back. Rawk drew in a deep breath and almost choked on the stench of death. It wasn't his death though, so that was a good thing. *Not today,* he muttered. *Tomorrow, probably.* He needed to find some help. He didn't look back either, as he left the alley. He kept his pace to a slow, measured walk. He kept his shaking hand on the hilt of his sword.

−O−

Rawk stepped into the foyer and smiled at Barin.

The big man smiled back. "Back again."

"I need to talk to some of your members."

"That sounds interesting." He pointed through the door in the left corner. "There's a common room and refectory through that direction. Probably the best place to find people who are willing to talk."

"I thought I might join first. Is that all right? I know I'm not a Veteran but..."

"You can join, but it will cost more than it does for a veteran and you don't get as many discounts. Through that way." He pointed to the door on the other side.

Rawk went where indicated, stepping through into a small office.

An attractive woman, about forty years old, sat behind a counter. She smiled when she saw him. "Rawk?" She rose to her feet and unconsciously straightened her hair. "My name is Maris. I didn't think I'd ever see you in here."

Rawk smiled back at her. "Well, Maris, my friend brought me the other day and I like the place. So I thought I might come a bit more often."

Maris smiled and straightened her dress as well, revealing just a little bit more cleavage in the process. "You like it?"

He nodded. "I'm liking it more all the time. So, what do I have to do to join?"

She pulled out a sheet of paper. "You have to fill this in... I could do that for you, if you just gave me the details."

"That would be wonderful. Thank you." He gave a silent sigh of relief. The writing looked very small. "You probably couldn't read my writing anyway."

When the forms were complete and Rawk had handed over ten ithel for one year's membership the woman concentrated on straightening her desk.

"Well, Maris, thank you for your help. I imagine I will be seeing you when I come to visit."

"Yes. I imagine. That would be nice. I mean..."

Rawk nodded and left with a single glance back. She was watching him. *Nice indeed.* He didn't spend a lot of time with women like Maris, with women as old as Maris, but he would be willing to make an exception.

Across the other side of the foyer he found himself in a wide, long hallway. Battle murals were painted on both walls, all the way from one end of the hall to the other. They were two stories high, life-sized, and the detail was stunning. Mud and blood. The glint of steel. Crows circling in the distance. A gaping wound here, a killing stroke there. A quiet moment of calm amidst the frenzy. A look of panic in a horse's eye, a look of resignation in a soldier's. Because they were so close— it was just a hallway and he couldn't get away— Rawk felt as if he was almost in the battle.

The silence was eerie. A battle should be noisy, deafening, the screams and the clash of weapons, the suck and squelch of mud underfoot, the wordless shouts. With the mural crowding his eyes the lack of noise was unsettling. It knocked him off balance, tripped him up as he looked nervously around. His hand rested on the hilt of *Dabaneera.*

At the first door on his left, Rawk was glad to step through into a refectory. On the right was a serving counter with half a dozen big pots sitting in a bed of hot coals. There were wooden bowls piled at one end and wooden spoons at the other. Near the latter was a huge pile of bread. Stew or stew for dinner, though at least there seemed to be a few to choose from. A man waited with a huge ladle and, near the spoons, a woman was taking money.

The lunch crowd had long gone, or else there had never been one, and only a dozen men occupied the thirty or so available tables as dinner crawled ever closer. A few more could be seen out on the porch that over looked the street.

Rawk looked at the two men sitting at the closest table and ruled them out. It looked as if they were veterans from the First Masaki War and probably hadn't picked up a sword for the last twenty years. The next table looked more promising. Rawk knew one of the three men sitting there, talking over their empty bowls.

"Galad," Rawk said, sitting in the spare seat a moment later. He slapped the other man on the back. "How's Heroism treating you?" Galad was good at the job. He was old enough to have been around before Weaver's new laws took effect.

He grunted. "Not as well as you, apparently."

"What do you expect if you sit around here all day?"

"I hardly sit around here. I got back in from Redami about two hours ago. I spent a week looking for a halanar and when I found it, it had already died of old age."

"What's wrong with that? An easy bounty."

"It would have been, except it died about two weeks earlier. More than long enough for it to be obvious."

"Oh."

"Exactly. 'Oh.' So I got nothing for my trouble. Then I get back home and discover I could have stayed here and had a wolden wolf and a troll."

Rawk held up two fingers.

"Two trolls?" Galad shook his head. "You always were a lucky bastard, Rawk."

"I make my own luck, Galad. They probably aren't trolls though. Duen giants, more likely. Who are your friends?"

"This is Fabi." He looked to be about same age as Galad—late thirties—with the dark skin of a southerner, a bald head and long beard. "He used to be in the army and now I'm just in the process of talking him out of taking up the Hero trade. And Thok." Thok was younger than the other two and looked as if he would struggle to string a complete sentence together. He was as big as a bear, almost as hairy, and seemed to wear a constant, bemused expression.

"So what do *you* do then, Thok?"

He shrugged. "This and that. Mainly work down on the wharves."

Rawk gave a nod and a smile. "Ever thought of following Galad here into the hero business?"

"No, I haven't. And no, I wouldn't."

"Just thought I'd ask because there may well be more duen in the forest."

That got Galad's attention. He sat up and rested his elbows on the table. "And why are you telling us this piece of news?"

"Well, Weaver is offering 3000 ithel for each duen that I kill so I thought you might—"

"Yes, but why are you telling us instead of going off to claim the bounty yourself?"

Rawk held up his arm and pulled up the sleeve of his shirt to reveal the bandages. He pulled up his shirt too. "I might be stupid," he said, "but not stupid enough to go back out there on my own. *One* of them did this to me. If I came across two or three..."

"You're forming a party?"

"That's right."

"How long's it been?"

"Nine years."

"That troop of malana..."

"Path, no. A bunch of others just followed me. Lazy bastards couldn't work anything out for themselves. It was a panamore up near Garn." He waved it away. "Anyway, are you interested?"

"Even split?"

Rawk gave it some thought. "A hundred off the top of each thousand for me, then an even split."

"A hundred off the top? Thirty."

Rawk sighed. "Let's just save time and go straight to sixty?"

"You've got to be... Oh. Right. Sixty sounds good."

"Thok?"

Thok shook his head. "I'm sure I've got something to do... whenever it is that this thing is happening."

"Fabi?"

"What happens if we find nothing?"

"Then we had a nice walk in the forest. And, Weaver said he'd pay a thousand for the effort."

Fabi grunted. "Three hundred and thirteen ithel for a walk in the forest?"

"Welcome to the life of a Hero."

"All right then. I'm in."

"Three?" asked Galad.

"Three it is."

"When?"

"Be up at the *Hero's Rest* at dawn."

The two men nodded.

"Now, I'm going to get something to eat," Rawk said. "Any recommendations?"

"I'm just going back to get some of the chicken stew," Fabi said.

Rawk followed him over to the counter. "You were fighting for Januze?" he asked, indicating the military tattoo on the other man's wrist.

"For about five years."

"Why'd you get out?"

"The King just keeps finding more wars. Each time, he somehow manages to come out on top but the wars are getting bigger. I figured his luck has to run out soon. I know the sensible part of his army is running out. As quick as they can."

Rawk nodded, wondering if he needed a bigger army himself. "Do you think Thok could be convinced to come with us tomorrow?"

"Not a chance. He's smart enough to know what's good for him and he doesn't do things that aren't good for him. Don't let his appearance fool you; he may well be the smartest man in Katamood."

"Really?"

"Thok isn't his real name. It means 'Wise One' in..." He shrugged, "Well, some language or other. And the name isn't used as a joke. Thok works on the wharves because he likes it. It gives him time to think, he says. But he was well on his way to following his father into banking before he had a change of heart."

"Banking? Well, can't blame him for wanting to get out of that."

"Exactly."

Back at the table. Rawk took a spoon full of stew. "So, you used to be in banking?" he said to Thok.

The other man nodded.

"You know about Maradon?"

Another nod.

"Has the country recovered from the revolt yet?"

Thok laughed. "Not yet. One season without crops and everything went to hell. I think, by now, the king realizes how important peasants really are. His epiphany just came a bit too late. They're close to getting back to where they were, but it will be a while yet."

Rawk ate his stew with the three men as afternoon turned into evening and the dinner crowd grew. Conversation shifted to other countries and other battles. Much later, when Galad was telling about the time be chased a verimal up Mount Higen, almost half way across the world, Rawk realized it had been years since he'd been away from Katamood for more than two or three days at a time. And each time he came back, he stayed for longer. He was getting old. Older by the day, it seemed.

Rawk cleared his throat. "Well, I'm going to bed. I'll see you at dawn."

Back out in the disturbing silence of the hall, Rawk stopped to looked one way and then the other, trying to ignore the mural. *Since I'm here*, he thought. He kept going the way he had been earlier, along the gauntlet of the mural. The next door led to a taproom, but it was almost overflowing with people, so he kept going. He turned at the end and a little further on he found himself in familiar territory. The Armory was as good a destination as any. He went down the stairs. There were a few men sitting in the dimness, more than the previous time, but it was still much quieter than upstairs. He bought an ale to nurse and found his way to the darkest corner.

Over the next half an hour the crowd grew until the room was full. When someone asked if they could share his table, Rawk thought it was time to leave. He half rose but stopped when the noise died away to a whisper and Celeste and Grint arrived on stage.

Rawk felt the power of the music even before they started to play. Two fermi–dwarf bastards were about to fill the room with a type of magic that Weaver would never eradicate. The knowledge of the music was enough to get his heart racing. Then Grint started to play on his drum, and a minute later, Celeste plucked the first note from the mandolin.

Two hours later, Rawk roused himself as Celeste bade her audience farewell in a quiet, nervous voice that seemed to come from some person other than the one who'd been singing. The room cleared quickly but Rawk stayed where he was, watching as Grint went to talk to the woman serving the drinks behind the bar. The two of them were still at it a few minutes later when Rawk rose to his feet and sauntered towards the stage.

Celeste sat on her stool, still and quiet, as she watched her brother. From the little he could hear, Rawk gathered it was about money but he didn't care.

He stopped near the stage and Celeste finally turned to look at him. She half smiled, looked down at her hands, suddenly fiddling in her lap. She had long fingers, rough and worn from hard work, and dark hair that clung to her head in tight curls, blending with her skin.

"Hello," he said.

She looked up at him and smiled fully. But she didn't answer. She looked back down at her hands and the folds of dress that they held.

Rawk opened his mouth to say something else, but he didn't know what he wanted to say. "I... You sing beautifully. And play." He gestured to the mandolin. Then thought he should mention Grint. "Your brother, too."

"Thank you, sir."

"I never thought a fermi or a dwarf could..."

She looked up at him then, met his eyes for one hard second, before looking away again. "We can do many things."

Rawk would have said more, tried to explain himself, perhaps, but at that moment Grint returned.

"She isn't going to pay us tonight," the dwarf said. "Says we'll get our money when the boss says we do."

"But what about—" Celeste looked at Rawk again for a moment. "That wasn't the agreement."

"You don't need to tell me, Celeste. But like she says, we can take it or leave it." Grint snatched up his drum and stalked out through the door behind the stage. Celeste followed a moment later.

Rawk stared at the door after it had closed.

"Bloody dwarf."

Rawk turned and saw the bar tender standing close behind.

"Comes in here and acts like he owns the place just because he can bang a drum."

"What was the agreement?" Rawk asked.

The woman shrugged. "It doesn't matter. He's only a dwarf."

"Of course. He should be happy he's even here."

"That's right." The woman looked around. "Anyway, it's time for me to pack up."

Rawk nodded. "I should be going, too."

Back up in the foyer, Rawk saw light coming from the offices where he had gone to join the Club earlier. He stuck his head around the corner and saw Maris still working behind the desk. He went in further and she looked up.

"You're working late," he said.

"I'm normally long gone by now but I just needed to finish up some things. It's been very busy here lately. I'm just about to head home though."

"That's where I'm heading, too." He smiled.

"Oh."

"So, where is it?"

"Pardon?"

"Where's your home?"

"Ummm..." Maris stilled her hands. "Does that normally work?" she asked. She looked up at him, as if the ridiculousness of the situation had relieved her of her nerves.

Rawk thought about that. He cleared his throat. "Yes."

Maris laughed. "Really? On who?"

"Well..." *On younger women.*

"You are attractive, Rawk." She looked him up and down. "Very attractive. And you are a legend; you are *Rawk*. But... I dream, like any woman, but it's been more than ten years since a nice smile and a silly line was enough to get me into bed."

"Right. Sorry."

Maris stood up. "I should be going."

"Of course." Rawk looked her up and down as well.

She caught him doing it and gave a small smile. A cheeky smile.

Rawk cleared his throat again, reluctant to let her walk out the door. "So are you going straight home?" he asked.

"It's late."

"Would you like a sugar stick?" Rawk laughed at the look on her face. "No, that isn't a euphemism. It's a desert."

"A desert?"

"Yes, it's... Well, if you want to know you'll just have to come with me."

"A sugar stick?"

"I'm not saying anything more."

Maris hesitated but gave a small nod.

Thersday

RAWK WOKE UP WHEN HE ALMOST fell off the chair. He sat up straighter and tried to work a crick out of his neck.

Maris was lying on the bed on the other side of the one small room that she called home. The first touch of dawn angled in through the only window, somehow finding its way between the buildings outside. The light painted her face and highlighting a scatter of freckles across her nose. She stirred as he watched, rolling onto her back and throwing up an arm to cover her eyes.

"Sorry I woke you," Rawk said.

She peeked out from behind her arm, as if only just realizing he was there. "Rawk?"

"Don't sound so surprised." Was she surprised he was still there, or surprised he'd been there at all?

"I just..." She looked around. "Why are you still here?"

"We were talking about Terunde City and..."

"I don't remember that."

"It was late. You suggested that I stay."

"I don't remember that either."

Maris sat up and examined her clothes. "I didn't get undressed."

Rawk had spent a couple of hours with a woman, come back to her place and everyone kept their clothes on. He smiled. Given the chance to go back, he wouldn't change a thing. "I've got to go," he said. "I'm going into the Old Forest to see if there are any more giants."

"Do you think there are?"

"Not really. But Weaver's paying me enough to go and look."

"Very well."

Rawk stood up, and hesitated. "So... Ahhh... I'll see you at the club or something?"

Maris said, "Yes," but the look on her face suggested she wouldn't be holding her breath.

"If not, you know where I live, right?"

"So, I should go to the *Hero's Rest* and find you?"

Had he just suggested that? When he thought about it, it seemed that he had. Actually, there wasn't any doubt at all. It had been a long while since something like that had happened.

Maris was older than most of the women he talked to. She was also more interesting than most of the women he talked to. Those two facts were most probably linked.

Rawk cleared his throat and took a deep breath. It felt as if he was setting himself for battle. "Yes, come and visit any time you like. I can't guarantee I'll be there, of course, but it won't be because I'm hiding."

Maris smiled and her face lit up. She was beautiful, but not like Adalee. She was a flower and the younger woman, the girl, was a necklace or some other contrived, ostentatious beauty.

Rawk smiled too. "But now, I really have to go." He quickly crossed the room to the bed and touched her cheek. He kissed her for the first time, lingering momentarily, tasting her lips. "I have to go." And he collected his sword from beside the door, hurrying out into the dooryard before he convinced himself he should stay.

Half a dozen dwarves grumbled their way past, heading for one job or another. A merchant pushed a barrow laden with vegetables. Rawk paid half an ithel for a radish and preceded the man up the hill.

At the top, he paused to look back over the city. His city. He thought he could almost see Maris' house. Or at least her street. Well, it was down there somewhere. He smiled and hurried into the courtyard at the side of the *Hero's Rest*. Galad had his feet up on a table and Fabi was looking through his pack.

Galad looked surprised. "You said you were going home to bed," he said.

"I never did. I said I was going to bed, but I didn't say whose it was." He wondered, for a moment, how Maris would feel about him playing with that truth.

"Was it worth it?"

"I'll be back in a minute." Rawk slipped in through the back door and went quickly up to his rooms. He changed his clothes and on his way back out the door he grabbed a dagger, his dwarven staff and a pack. In the kitchen, Kalesie was already working, pounding at dough to make the day's bread as a big pot of stew bubbled over the stove. The others wouldn't be too far away.

"Have you got something I can take, Kalesie?" Rawk asked the woman.

"Take where?" She didn't stop working. She didn't even look up.

"Into the Old Forest."

"There's some bread left from yesterday. And some cheese and salty beef in the cooler."

Rawk found the food, filched a couple of apples and collected his waterskin from the hook behind the door. He started to go outside, so he could fill it from the barrel by the door, but stopped. He turned to the washtub beneath the window.

"Have you used the tap yet?" he asked.

Kalesie finally stopped working and turned to look as well. "That thing? Path, no. I don't trust dwarves and I don't trust that."

"It's just a tap." But Rawk had to force himself to go over to the tub where the tap waited like a viper ready to strike. "There's just a pipe and..."

"I saw the dwarf that put the thing in there. He was a shifty little bugger if ever I saw one. He was blind in one eye, you know."

"It's just a tap." He reached out hesitantly and turned the tap. Cool, clear water flowed into the tub and down the drain the dwarf had cut in the base. Rawk watched it for a moment then filled his skin. "It's just a tap."

"If you say so."

"It would be silly to not use it." He turned it off quickly.

Kalesie didn't look sure. Rawk left her staring at the offending object and headed back outside.

"A minute, you said," Galad said as he hurried over.

"Stop complaining. Come on."

Galad and Fabi both had bows resting against the table near by. They collected them and their packs and rushed to follow Rawk out onto the street.

It was still early but a crowd was growing before they'd gone a hundred yards. Galad waved and smiled though he must have known they weren't there for him.

"Where are you going, Rawk?" someone called.

"Are there more trolls?"

By the time they reached the wall, there were at least fifty people following along behind. That was bigger than usual these days, but it wasn't hard for them to work out that something was going on. Rawk stopped on the top of the wall and raised his hands. "We don't know if there are more trolls," he said. "We are going to see."

"Are we being invaded?"

"We are *not* being invaded. There is nothing to worry about. If there are trolls, and they get past us, then the City Guard will be able to handle them."

"Make sure you kill all of them, Rawk. I don't want a troll coming into my house. My mother doesn't stop worrying about them."

"Tell her there's nothing to worry about. Now, we must go, before Prince Weaver calls out Hawk Squad again and they steal all my glory."

Rawk waved and the crowd cheered. Galad and Fabi waved as well and there was more cheering. The two of them were smiling as they scrambled down the far side of the wall.

"Is it always like that, Rawk?" Fabi asked.

He nodded. "It's a bit annoying sometimes." He realized it was annoying most of the time. When had that happened?

—O—

In the forest, Rawk found the half−trail he'd followed last time and led the way into the ruins of the city. They walked in silence for some time, moving along grassy streets, stepping through the buildings.

When they reached the place where Rawk had killed the duen, there was nothing to see. The flowers in the house had been crushed but the remains of the creature had gone. Rawk didn't know if they had been removed by Weaver's men or by something else. He looked around but could see no evidence to suggest either way.

"So, where to now?" Fabi asked.

Rawk looked up. "North−west, I suppose. Further in." And he rubbed at his knee. He'd forgotten to put the cream on and it was starting to hurt as well. But his left arm wasn't too bad. He had to admit, Sylvia, Silver Lark, was a good healer. Possibly even better than Janas. But then elves were like that. It was hard to get them to do physical work, but they reveled in anything involving study or learning. Give them a library and they were as happy as pigs in mud. He grunted. "Come on. Let's see what we can find."

Galad took a moment to string his bow and moved his quiver of arrows to a more accessible position.

"I can't believe you use a bow, Galad." Rawk stepped back out of the house and continued down the street.

Galad shook his head. "I can't believe you're still alive."

"Back in the old days a Hero wouldn't be caught dead with a bow."

"And how many of those old Heroes are left, Rawk? Just you?" He hefted the weapon. "Maybe if some of those old timers had a bow they'd still be alive today."

"Maybe," Rawk conceded, "but if we all carried bows then nobody would've cared. Anyone can shoot a creature from fifty paces away. Where's the skill in that? Where's the romance?"

"Have you ever tried shooting a bird on the wing? Two birds? Ten? Or a mushon? There is skill involved, let me assure you."

"You killed a mushon?"

Galad smiled and held up three fingers.

"Three?" Four times in his life, Rawk had walked away from a commission. Three of those had been for a mushon.

"They were down near Grinport. Harassing a little village just to the east. Even took a child."

Rawk grunted. That was one of the ones he'd turned down. If he'd known there were three of them he would've run even quicker.

"The last one was about five yards from me when I got it. They taste like chicken."

"Really?"

"I have a cloak at home made from their skins. Even now, the colors shift and change and blend with the background. It's hanging on the back of the door and half the time I don't even realize it's there."

"That must be worth..."

"Exactly."

"You leave it hanging on the back of the door?"

"No thief will even know it's there. But why are you even talking about my bow? You have a staff, like an old man. Or a wizard or something."

"Don't knock the staff. I used it to stab the last duen."

The further they went, the thicker the crowd of trees on the street became. A gentle breeze whispered all around. Rawk half expected to come across the King of Trees, holding audience before his adoring public. But there were just more trees and more crumbling skeletons of buildings. Once or twice they even came across a house or business that seemed to be almost intact. One two-story building was missing only a roof. Though perhaps the vines that clung to the walls were all that held it up.

There was no king, and no adoring crowds, but the forest still watched. A gentle breeze whispered through the leaves. *"What are they doing here?"*, *"Come look, warriors are among us"*. It was cool under the trees, but whenever Rawk stepped into a patch of sunlight he felt his skin tingling.

Half an hour later, they crossed a major road and stepped into a place where the trees were huge and the buildings non—existent.

"What just happened?" Fabi asked.

They all stopped to look around.

"Did we leave the city?"

Galad shook his head. "I don't think so."

Rawk didn't think so either. The city already seemed huge, but he felt as if they should have been approaching the center, not stepping back out into the wilderness. He looked back the way they'd come. "Maybe it's a park."

"Right. So, do we keep going? Or do we go back and go around the outside?"

"Let's go back and see what we can see."

They returned to the road then turned north. They followed the edge of whatever—it—was for a few hundred yards, trees on one side, city on the other, without seeing anything much at all. There were birds and squirrels and even a fox, but that didn't help. There were no trails and no clues.

"Do we go and check the other direction?"

Fabi laughed and looked at the taller trees. "Let's get it over with. We all know that's most likely where the things will be."

Rawk didn't say anything. He hefted his pack, and followed the other man into the trees. It was slow going as they hacked and barged their way forward. It was noisy too. Not the best way to go about things, but Rawk didn't want to spend the next week wandering around the forest.

A hundred yards in, Fabi waved a signal. Rawk had never been in the army, but he knew enough to stop in his tracks. He cocked his head to listen. Dogs. They might have been normal dogs but he didn't like the odds of that. He drew *Dabaneera* and crouched down by the side of a tall, rough barked tree that he didn't recognize. And they waited.

Five minutes later, the dogs were still barking, but they didn't seem to be getting any closer.

"How long do we wait?" Galad asked.

Rawk remembered fighting the one dog. It hadn't been fun. And now it sounded as if there were a dozen of them, all baying for his blood.

"Let's rest here for a minute. Have something to eat."

"Are you getting old, Rawk?"

"I'm getting *hungry*." Rawk rummaged through his pack and found something to eat then sat with his back against the tree and his boots in a thin, dusty shaft of sunlight. "Everyone keeps telling me I'm getting old," he said eventually, when his bread and one of the apples was gone. "They keep telling me to grow up."

"And what do you say to them?" Fabi was eating an apple too, crunching all the way through the core.

"I don't say anything," Rawk said. "I go and find another monster to kill." But who was he trying to convince? "Come on." He rose to his feet, flexed his knee, and headed towards the sound.

It took an hour to move half a mile further into the forest. They went from tree to tree, stopping to listen to the baying of the dogs. They waded across a stream and followed a narrow, snaking ravine for a hundred yards, glad of the cover but wary of something jumping on them from above. The ground climbed the whole way.

The further they went, the more rocks there were. They climbed a rocky knoll and could see more and more of the outcrops ahead of them, breaking through the trees like small islands above the waves. And slightly to the north, a thin stream of smoke licked at the air.

Rawk's mouth was suddenly dry. He took a long drink from his water skin, wiping his mouth on the back of his hand. "Well, I guess we know where we're going," he said.

The others didn't reply.

He climbed back down and changed course.

−O−

Rawk froze when he saw the first of the dogs. He didn't signal, but Galad and Fabi knew something was wrong because they stopped too, sharing a glance before sinking down to hide amongst the undergrowth. Rawk put a hand against a tree to steady himself and waited to see what would happen. The creature watched him, white fur bristling, but it didn't come any closer. There were others, barking and growling, but Rawk couldn't see them. There were at least four.

When the dog stayed put, Rawk stalked forward, pausing between each step to make sure he wasn't being set up. But the barking stayed in front of him and nothing came from any other direction. Finally, he came to the edge of a clearing and he crouched down too. Six dogs in total, all bigger than the first one he had killed. Each was tied to the stump of a tree by a length of rope as thick as Rawk's arm. And in the middle of the clearing, made from the trees, stood a cabin. Or maybe it was a meeting hall for it was large enough to fit two score men. It was ten yards long and half that wide. The only visible window stared blankly from two yards above the ground.

Rawk beckoned to the others and they stalked forward.

"Is anyone home?" Fabi whispered.

"I don't know."

"Maybe the two you killed were the only ones who live here and the dogs are just getting hungry."

But a booming voice came from inside the cabin. When the dogs didn't stop barking, a huge duen, even bigger than the others Rawk had fought, came around the corner of the building. It was a female, covered in long grey fur and wearing a robe that went over one shoulder and wrapped around the waist. She held the biggest frypan Rawk had ever seen.

Rawk froze. He held his breath. The duen stopped near the corner of the building and said something to the dogs, but it was staring into the trees. After a few seconds, it went to one of the dogs and released it from its tether.

The dog bounded forward, growling and barking.

Fabi stood up quickly and fired his bow. Galad followed suit a moment later and the two arrows thudded into the chest of the beast. The duen stared for a moment, then cried out. She took a step towards the fallen dog, then changed direction and went to the next dog in line instead. Fabi fired again, at the duen this time. The creature didn't appear to be watching, but it spun and swatted away the shaft with the frypan. She shouted, "Hold," at the dog as she released it. It stayed close to her side, teeth bared, eager to leap forward. The duen saved it, deflecting another arrow from Galad. Then she released the next dog with the same command. The dogs followed her to the next tree stump and waited for her to untie the next dog.

"Get the dogs that are still tied," Rawk shouted to his companions. "She's keeping them close so she can protect them."

Four arrows whisked out in quick succession. One dog died with two shafts in its throat. Another was struck in the leg but didn't seem concerned. The duen knocked aside the final arrow as she released the fourth dog, leaving the injured one where it was. Then she shouted another command and the dogs scattered, running towards the cover of the trees. When they were safe, the duen backed towards the corner of the building, frypan at the ready.

When she had gone from sight, Rawk drew *Dabaneera*. "Path. What do we do now?" He examined the forest but could see no sign of the dogs. They were out there somewhere and it would be hard for Galad and Fabi to get a clean shot.

"Where is safer?" Fabi asked. "In here we have some cover but so do they. Out there..."

"I'm going out there," Rawk said. If he could get his back against the wall of the cabin before the duen returned... If it intended to return. Perhaps she had fled with the dogs, going for help.

But Fabi fired an arrow into the trees. He plucked another arrow from his quiver and fired again. Galad fired as well.

"Three to go," Fabi said.

Rawk's heart raced. He shifted his grip on his sword and tried to see everywhere at once. He had to stop himself from twirling on the spot, spinning from one slight sound to another. They were in a forest, the world was full of sounds that could be a charging dog or a clumsy squirrel or a branch in the breeze.

Another dog came from nowhere. Fabi reacted quickly. He stepped to the side, ducked, but was still knocked from his feet. Before the beast could leap away, Galad put an arrow in its flank. It staggered and Rawk darted forward to finish it off. He slipped *Dabaneera* into its stomach and up under its ribs.

"Two to go," Fabi said through clenched teeth. He hauled himself to his feet, clutching his right shoulder. "Someone else can be the bait next time."

"Let's get to the cabin."

"I'll cover you," Fabi said, collecting his bow from where he'd dropped it.

Rawk didn't know if Fabi could draw the bow but wasn't about to ask. He would just pretend he could and be happy for it. Galad darted away from the trees while Rawk followed. Once they had their backs against the wall, they turned and Galad pulled out his bow as Fabi crossed the open space.

A dog came from the trees, silent, head low, ears back. Rawk dropped into a fighting crouch as an arrow whisked out from beside him. The dog staggered but kept coming. Fabi hardly seemed to be moving. The dog was right there. Another arrow hit it in the chest and it fell to the ground like an avalanche. It knocked Fabi from his feet and Rawk went out to drag him over to the wall. His knee struggled to bare the extra weight. "Path," He muttered. "I should be at home." *Or even better, I should be at Maris' home, lying in the sun.* He tried to calm his racing heart.

"One to go," Galad said, breathing heavy.

Plus one still tied up. Rawk was about to suggest they finish the injured creature off, but never got the chance.

The duen came around the corner, sword in one hand, small, round shield in the other. Small for her. It seemed to be the size of a dinner table. She paused, looking at the dead dogs, then stalked forward again.

"You will pay for the death of my dogs."

Rawk set himself as Fabi tried to draw his bow. As suspected, the other man grunted in pain and gave it up as too hard. Galad fired, but the duen knew how to use the shield. She knocked the arrow aside and kept coming. Rawk went to meet her. He ducked under one experimental swing and lunged forward, careful of his knee, trying to ignore his arm. But the shield came around and almost knocked him from his feet. He went with the blow and found himself in the open and within range of the still-tied dog.

"Galad." He darted back towards the building just as the dog attacked and Galad fired another arrow. The creature yelped, staggered and fell to the ground. The duen called out and Rawk used *Dabaneera* to slide a blow over the top of his head. For a moment he thought his arm might be broken.

"Another one."

"What?"

But when he turned around he could see for himself. Another duen came around the building from the other direction. Galad fired again, but the newcomer turned the shaft aside.

"Path." Galad threw down his bow and drew his sword. "What have you gotten us into, Rawk?"

Rawk rolled under an attack. "Six thousand ithel, that's what." He swung his own attack, but the duen was somewhere else. "You help Fabi."

Fabi had his sword out but it wasn't obvious if he had the strength to use it. His arm hung limply at his side. The bruising was obvious through his torn shirt. But at the last moment, as the second duen moved in, he swapped his sword to his left hand and attacked. The move was so unexpected that he almost succeeded. But the creature parried the blow and retreated quickly. Fabi kept up the attack and Galad rushed forward to help.

Rawk narrowly avoided having his head removed and tried to concentrate. He fell back, rolled and came to his feet out in the open again. He had a quick look around for the final dog but it was nowhere in sight. Then the duen was on him again and he didn't have time to worry. He dodged, swung wildly and almost fell over a tree stump. Still on his feet, just, he scrambled away.

When he had his balance he stopped and readied himself. The duen advanced, sword low. Rawk wasn't quite sure what he should do. If he kept doing what he was doing he would make a mistake sooner rather than later. It wouldn't take much. A trip, a decision made a moment too late. His knee finally locking up. Life always hung on such things but the duen made him think about it for the first time in a long time. The creature was big and fast. It had a long reach. It had a shield. He glanced at Fabi and Galad.

They were having more luck than he was. With two of them attacking, the second duen had a hard time keeping up. It spun one way and the next, somehow managing to keep the two men at bay.

Rawk had just decided to wait until somebody could come to help when the duen came at him hard. Perhaps she'd had the thought that her friend needed help and the only way she could provide that was if Rawk was dead. Rawk blocked and dodged. He swung *Dabaneera* low and missed by more than a foot.

He would be lucky to reach her, even if he found an opening.

The duen pushed forward again and Rawk clambered up onto a tree stump to give himself more height. It sounded like a good plan for a moment, but he needed to dodge and couldn't even take a step without falling back to the ground. Once, he would have done a somersault to get back down. Now, he should've known better than to get up there in the first place. He jumped one swing, clanging his sword against the duen's shield in reply, then leapt down to the ground. His knee screamed at him and this time it wouldn't hold his weight. He fell to the ground in a heap, clutching his leg with one hand and his sword with the other. He couldn't think.

The duen was on him in a second, sword raise for the killing stroke. Rawk could see it through his haze of pain but he knew there was nothing he could do. He tried to forget his knee and raise his sword anyway. He was successful, little good that it would do.

The duen gave a small, sad smile. Rawk watched as she started to...

The creature flinched, half turned and Rawk followed her gaze. There was someone behind her. It was such an incongruous sight that Rawk wasn't sure he was really seeing it.

The dwarf hardly came to her waist, but he had a dagger and poked and prodded at her hamstring for all he was worth. It was like a wasp stinging an elephant, but the attack distracted the duen for a moment and allowed Rawk to gain his feet. Before he could do more, the duen swung her shield and the edge caught the dwarf in the side of the head. His feet left the ground and his head crashed into the tree stump Rawk had recently vacated. The was a dull thud, like a watermelon hitting the road.

Rawk should have attacked then, but he was stunned. He stared at the still figure of the dwarf, wondering where he had come from, wondering what had happened, and then the moment had passed. He staggered backwards as the duen rounded on him. It followed, attacking high, then low. Rawk slid the first blow aside, jumped the second. He managed to keep his feet when the duen made use of the shield again. The wind rushed from his lungs. He wheezed, struggled to stay upright as his opponent pressed the advantage. He could barely raise his sword.

And at that moment, Galad screamed. It was a strange, gurgling sound that was followed a moment later by a bellow of pain from the second duen.

Rawk looked across to the other fight. Galad was on the ground, hand held to his neck as blood gushed out. If he still lived, it was a miracle.

But the duen had been injured as well. Fabi had buried his sword in its stomach. Blood, much darker than Galad's, ran down the hilt and dripped onto the ground.

The female cried out, turned, took half a step, paused. Rawk watched for a moment before realizing this was his last chance. He limped forward while the creature was distracted and swung *Dabaneera* with all his strength. The razor sharp edge bit into the duen's side. She called out, but Rawk twisted the blade to open up the wound. When she reached down, groping blindly, he let go of the hilt and backed away. She stood for a moment, blood coating her hands and legs, pulsing out onto the ground, then collapsed. Rawk sank to the ground as well.

"Are you all right, Fabi?" he asked. He wasn't sure if the other man would be able to hear him.

"I'll live."

Which was more than could be said for Galad. And the dwarf.

Rawk didn't look at either of them. There would be time for thinking about that later. He didn't want to think at all. He just wanted to sit and breathe for a while. Instead, he rose painfully to his feet, pulled *Dabaneera* free of the duen's body, and staggered around to the other side of the cabin.

"Where are you going?"

"There may be more. There may be..." He didn't know what else there may be.

The door to the cabin was open and he went through, sword at the ready. There was a huge table, half prepared meal on the freshly planed boards. There were vegetables and roots hanging in bunches from the roof near a fire pit with a trickle of smoke searching for the chimney. At one end, straw was spread around inside a wooden frame and at the other end three beds had been attached to the wall.

And that was all.

Rawk returned to the scene of the fight and slumped down beside Fabi. He wiped sweat from his face. He flexed his injured arm.

"So?" Fabi asked, looking at his sword as if the last thing he wanted to do was get back to his feet to use it.

"Nothing. And this is the last of them, I think."

"Why?"

Rawk gestured vaguely. "There are four beds."

A crow fluttered down from a tree and landed on one of the stumps. It stretched its wings then settled down to watch.

"That damn crow is following me," Rawk said.

Fabi looked. "Are you sure?"

"Yes."

"How?"

"It's the same one." Rawk threw a stick at it. The bird didn't even move as the stick sailed harmlessly past. "It's big and black and has beady eyes. It looks exactly the same."

"Well, as long as you're sure."

Rawk wanted to throw something else, but there couldn't reach any suitable ammunition.

"So, we go home now?" Fabi asked eventually.

"I guess so."

"And Galad?"

It looked like Galad was still in pain. His face was twisted, his hand still clutched at his neck trying to hold in the blood. His face was pale, too pale, his mouth open in a silent scream. He would still be alive if Rawk hadn't spotted him sitting in the refectory. He'd be siting somewhere right now, maybe telling someone about the three mushon he'd killed.

Rawk looked at the body. "He was a good man."

He hadn't really realized how good until the day before, sitting with him in the Veteran's Club, drinking and talking. It had been the first time he'd ever seen him as anything other than a rival. It was the first time he'd thought about the man behind the Hero. He'd liked him. Maybe they could've been friends. Rawk gave a bark of laughter and realized how it might sound. He tried to explain, without explaining, before Fabi could even ask the question.

"What happened isn't funny," he said. "But..." He shrugged. "It's strange how life travels along nicely for so long, then decides to slap you in the face, a lot, just when you least expect it."

"Yes. Strange. I suppose." Fabi obviously didn't care about the details. "And speaking of strange." He gestured towards the dwarf with his chin.

Rawk tore his eyes away from Galad, away from the slowly growing pool of blood, and looked at the dwarf. "I have no idea who that is or where he came from."

Fabi nodded.

"He saved my life."

Fabi's eyes narrowed. "Him? He's just a dwarf."

"I know." It was crazy. Crazy that the dwarf was even here, and crazy that he would attack the duen with a dagger. The creature was literally twice his size.

Fabi crawled to the dwarf and started going through his pockets. The first thing he found was a small block of paper sheets. He looked at the top one, then threw it to Rawk.

Rawk looked. There was writing... "He works for the damn newspaper thing."

"Are you sure?"

"Someone's been following me, writing about everything I do." He looked at the dwarf again. He didn't look any different to any of the others. Just a dwarf.

"I've read some of those stories."

"They aren't true." He read some of the drawf's scrawled notes. They stuck to the facts and ended mid battle. Mid sentence. "Well, not everything."

"So now what?"

Rawk sighed. "I saw a shovel inside."

"You want to bury Galad out here?"

He nodded. "And the dwarf."

"You want to bury the dwarf?"

"Are you up to carrying them back to Katamood? Either of them?"

Fabi checked his shoulder, working it gently. "Don't think so."

"Well, me either." He pushed himself to his feet.

"We can just do one though. We don't have to worry about the dwarf."

Rawk looked at the dwarf and sighed. "He saved my life." It wouldn't have to be a very big hole anyway. This was probably the type of place Galad would like to rest. Quiet and green. Peaceful. And the dwarf deserved to be there with him.

Faraday

RAWK SAT DOWN. He was dressed in nothing more than a towel and used that to wipe his hand so he could pick up the *Encyclopedia of Myth* from the floor by the chair. With the book in his lap, he closed his eyes and sat while he simply enjoyed breathing.

A few minutes later, he flicked through the pages until he found the right one.

"Duen giants are said to have roamed the lands north of Manapee more than two thousand years ago. Wherever they went, violence followed. It is suggested they were almost constantly involved in conflicts, across the breadth of the continent, including the Battle of Hapahide and the Siege of Makanua Rock that was remembered in the famous folk song of the same name. It seems they were nomadic, presumably in order to find more enemies to battle."

He examined the two pictures for a moment, then turned the page. The picture of the girl stared back at him.

"Not much is known about the duen but it is possible they lived in large clan or family groups that acted as separate units in battle. It seems the children were kept aside, protected from the fighting."

Rawk grunted. *Not much is known, but let's speculate anyway...*

There was a knock at the door.

"Yes."

"You're all wet," Travis said when he came in.

"I had a shower."

"Really? So it doesn't scare you any more?"

"It *never* scared me," Rawk said. He knew Travis didn't believe him.

"Anyway, you've got a visitor."

"Fabi?"

"Who?"

"Big black guy with a beard?"

"That's him. Did he go with you yesterday?"

Rawk nodded.

"Hubb was here too, for a while."

"Did he want to see me?"

"Not sure. He had some breakfast but then people started challenging him to arm wrestle."

Rawk grunted. "He never gets a break, apparently. When people see him they expect him to drop everything so they can validate their manhood or something."

"I wouldn't imagine many of them would leave feeling validated."

"Not that I've seen." He decided he wasn't going to get time to rest. The cream for his knee was under the chair. "I'll be down in a minute."

"I'll let Fabi know." Travis slipped out the door.

Rawk rubbed the cream on and, once he was done, dressed and made his way downstairs. Fabi was sitting at the bar.

"How are you feeling?" Rawk asked.

"I've been better."

Rawk nodded. "Me too. Come on, then. Let's get this over with."

But in the end he suggested Fabi wait in the square while he went in to see Weaver on his own.

"You aren't trying to rip me off, are you?" Fabi said it like a joke, but he was probably worried it was the truth.

"Of course not. It's just that I can win an argument with Weaver, but witnesses would make it a lot more difficult."

"Oh, right then."

"I won't be long."

Rawk entered through the guardroom to the right of the main gate. He waved to the men as he went through but didn't pause.

The public areas of the palace were ostentatious, as those things normally were. Brocaded drapes that hid the plain stone walls. Artifacts from all around the world— gold, silver, ivory, silk, ebony, diamonds—stood on tables or shelves on the walls. If someone, sometime, had thought it was valuable, Weaver probably had it in the palace somewhere.

The contrast with the private areas was stark. Beyond the five Guards and the stout wooden door, the plain stone walls were sparsely adorned with weapons and simple tapestries. There were suits of armor, shields and trophies taken from vanquished foe. A banner, a tunic, a helm with a slice through the crown.

Rawk made his way to Weaver's private chambers. A Guard at the door knocked then let him through at a call from beyond. The room was the same as the passages outside, only more so. Every inch of wall seemed to be covered with something. There was a shield Rawk had used for a while many years earlier. There was a cloak he'd taken from a Habon prince. There were broken weapons and weapons that could have no practical purpose.

"Rawk. Good to see you." Weaver stood by his desk, shirtless and disheveled as if he'd just gotten out of bed.

Rawk sat down in his usual chair. It was a plain wooden thing, hard and uncomfortable. He grunted.

"So, to what do I owe the pleasure?"

"Galad is dead," he said, quietly.

Weaver looked shocked. "He is? Well, that was about the last thing I expected you to say."

Sitting on the chair, Rawk wondered about expectations. The front of the palace was gaudy and bright because that was what people expected. But back here was the opposite, because *that* was what people expected as well. Prince Weaver, the ex−Hero. Prince Weaver, the common man. Rawk wondered which one was true. He wondered if even Weaver knew any more.

The Prince sat down in his chair, eager for the story. "You found more trolls? Did one kill Galad?"

And Rawk decided he'd had enough. He'd had enough of everything that was expected of him. His knee ached. His arm was a constant burning pain. His back popped and creaked when he moved. He wanted to rest. He wanted to... He didn't know what he wanted. But he knew he didn't want to sit here telling stories about the death of a good man to please Weaver. And the dwarf. Weaver would brush the dwarf's death aside. Or maybe the dwarf would become a man in years to come. Nobody wanted a dwarf to save the Hero.

And the duen. Rawk remembered the picture in the book and the girl in the forest. The look on her face when she saw the collar. The look on her face when she died. Had he killed a child who was out looking for her pet?

"No," Rawk said eventually. "There were no more trolls." He wondered if the duen actually liked arm wrestling at all. Or did they do it simply because people expected them to?

"None?"

He cleared his throat. "We went in but..."

"You found nothing?" Weaver sat back, disappointed.

"Nothing at all."

"Then how...?"

"A tree fell on him."

"Galad died when a tree fell on him?"

"Yes. Stupid, I know. After all he'd been through... He killed three mushon, you know?"

"I didn't know that."

"I only found out yesterday myself."

"He was one of the good ones. Not up to your standard, obviously, but... He was good."

Rawk nodded.

"So... I've reported. Now I'd like my one thousand ithel, plus the money for the stuff I did kill."

"What? Oh, yes, of course. Three thousand one hundred ithel all together, right?"

"Oh, there's also the fire sprite."

Weaver sighed. "A small elemental? Two hundred, if I remember correctly."

"And a kitten."

"I heard about the demon kitten. I can't pay you for it though because you let it escape."

"Nothing gets past you, does it?" Rawk had to sit and wait while Weaver went to organize things. He sat with his eyes closed and tried not to think. But it wasn't easy.

Weaver came back a few minutes later carrying a full purse. "It's all there," he said.

Rawk weighed it in his hand.

"Do you trust me?"

"I'll be on my way, I guess."

"Very well. Thank you for your efforts." Weaver clasped his hand. "It's been good to see you back in action, Rawk. It's just like old times, isn't it?"

"Something like that." He had the *old* bit right.

"Are you claiming Galad's possessions?"

"Does he have any family?"

"Not that I know of."

Rawk nodded. "Then I am. But I'll leave it for a while, so let me know if someone else claims as well."

"He was buying the rooms he lived in. Paper work came through about a month ago."

"Tell me about it when we see if anyone turns up."

Fabi was waiting at the edge of the park but before he could make his way to the other man, Rawk felt a touch on his elbow.

"Hello, Rawk."

"Janas?" He looked around, wondering if someone was playing a joke. "But... You died."

The old lady laughed. "Of course not. My sister did though. I've been over in Westport with her family." She smiled a gap toothed smile. "I hear you've been busy. Are you all right?"

"Yes. A few aches and pains, but..." He shrugged.

"Well, come and see me this afternoon, if you like."

Rawk cleared his throat. "I've actually found a new healer—"

"A new healer? But what's wrong with the old one?"

Rawk cleared his throat. "I heard that she died."

"Well, I didn't."

"Sorry, Janas. Things change."

"Not for you, Rawk. Not for the last twenty years."

"The world moves on. We move on. And sometimes it's hard to tell which is which."

Janas grunted and spat on the ground. It looked like she was going to say something, but she stormed off without uttering another word.

Shaking his head, Rawk crossed the road.

Fabi was sitting on a stone wall that surrounded an ancient oak tree. "Who was that?"

"Janas. She used to be my healer."

"I heard she died."

"Me too."

Fabi stared after her for a moment. "Well, did Weaver pay?"

Rawk nodded. He put the purse in the other man's lap.

"All of it?"

"There's 3300 ithel in there for you. And he's going to give us a bit extra in a few days."

"Why?"

"He wants us to keep quiet about the duen because he doesn't want anyone to know there were more of them."

"We aren't allowed to say anything?"

Rawk winced. "No. Sorry."

"But..."

"I know. You want to be a Hero and Heroes need publicity." Rawk looked across the square at the *Hero's Rest*. It looked much as it had for a long time, except for the tank on the roof, but it seemed different, like a boat drifting away from shore. "You should find some other work. A different type of work, I mean. Become a fisherman. Or a butcher."

"Fighting is all I know."

Rawk nodded. "Still." He shrugged. "Become a body guard for a rich merchant, if you must, but not this. Not this. The money will help you get set up."

"So, are you retiring then?"

Rawk laughed. "I retired a couple of days ago. Don't tell anyone about it though because, with all these exots around, I think neither Weaver nor the world is going to let me get away."

Fabi didn't say anything.

"I'll see you around, Fabi? You know where to find me if you want a drink? I'd like to have a drink with you."

"Of course." He shook the purse. "It will be my shout."

"Even if you don't want a drink, come and visit anyway. Apparently I don't have a lot of friends, so..."

"That's probably because people never consider being friends with a legend. They expect you to be too important for the likes of them."

Rawk nodded and gave a small smile. "Things aren't always as you expect."

He took a strip of meat from the pouch on his belt and headed for home.

Keep an eye out for the continuing adventures of Rawk in
The Last Great Hero Book 2:
A History of Magic.

Please help support
independent writers and publishers.
Your money is wonderful.
So are your reviews,
comments, mentions, tweets,
emails, blogs, likes
and deliveries of chocolate.

ABOUT THE AUTHOR

Scott J. Robinson grew up in a small town in rural Australia, the kind of place where you had to make your own fun. And from a young age, his idea of fun was to create strange worlds and populate them with interesting people.

He now lives in a different small town, with his wife and three children, and still enjoys creating strange worlds. Though now, he actually finishes some of the things he starts. When not writing he enjoys photography and camping and recently retired from an amazingly mediocre cricket career.

For more information visit
www.tengama.com
or email
scott@tengama.com

Other books by Scott J. Robinson

Tribes of the Hakahei
Book 1: The Space Between
Book 2: Singing Other Worlds
Book 3: The Time Comes
Book 4: A Different Kind of Heaven

Kim McLean is just another tourist visiting Sherwood Forest when aliens attack on the back of giant bats. She didn't think her day could get much weirder after that, until she follows an elf and a dwarf through a magical gateway to another world.

Then, as the endless alien hordes keep coming, she gets involved with bureaucrats and soldiers, governments and people who should know better, and she starts to wonder if her definition of weird needs to be revised.

All she knows for sure is that it's up to her to save the human race.

Travelling to distant worlds and different universes, she gathers strange companions and uncovers long forgotten secrets as she tries to end the death and destruction.

But the war was being waged long before Sherwood Forest was attacked and Kim soon suspects that they aren't even fighting the right enemy.

The Brightest Light

Kade was once the up and coming star of The Skyway Men, a ruthless criminal organization. Then he made one mistake. Then another. Then one too many. Lucky to be left alive, he was banished to a backwoods skyland that flew the quietest wind–lanes.

When he's finally offered another chance Kade can't believe his luck.

But ten years working a smithy and fixing crystal engines is a long time, and with a weapon like none other up for grabs, the stakes are higher than ever.

In a world of death and corruption, shady deals and dirty deeds Kade doesn't know who to trust. He doesn't know who's on which side. He doesn't even know which side *he's* on any more.

All he knows is that in a world of kill or be killed he suddenly isn't sure which is the better option.

www.ingramcontent.com/pod-product-compliance
Lightning Source LLC
Chambersburg PA
CBHW020612120726
47905CB00003B/769